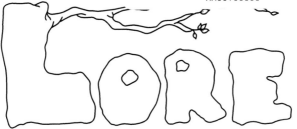

a quaint and curious volume of selected stories

Edited by
Rod Heather and Sean O'Leary

Published by The LORE Firm, LLC
Haddonfield, New Jersey

www.lore-online.com

LORE: A Quaint and Curious Volume of Selected Stories
Published by The LORE Firm, LLC, Haddonfield, New Jersey

ISBN: 978-0-9847730-0-8

This edition is dedicated to my father,
Rod Heather, Sr.

— Rod

For Mom and Dad, for Monica, and,
of course, for Monty.

— Sean

ACKNOWLEDGEMENTS

The editors would like to thank the following people, without whose support, this volume would not be possible:

Robert Feldman, Kathleen Horwedel, Derrick Hussey, S.T. Joshi, Philip Nobile Jr., John Picinich, Robert M. Price, Angelo 'Buz' Marino, Joseph Martucci, and Jeffrey Thomas.

CHARNEL KNOWLEDGE

"I THINK IT WOULD BE FUN TO RUN A NEWSPAPER."

Remember that line from *Citizen Kane*? It's from a letter the young, 25-year-old Charles Foster Kane writes to his business manager, Mr. Thatcher, wherein he responds to Thatcher's insistence that Kane cease his traveling and take responsibility for his various and considerable business concerns. Kane informs Thatcher that he is "not interested in gold mines, oil wells, shipping or real estate." However, there is one item, and one item only, on his extensive list of holdings that interests Kane: a seemingly insignificant acquisition, a not-terribly-successful newspaper called the New York Inquirer. Kane assures his return to the U.S. at once to take control of the paper, signing off with, "I think it would be fun to run a newspaper."

Thatcher bristles at the frivolity!

There are no commonalities between the story of LORE and *Citizen Kane* other than that, as we sit here in 2011 and look back sixteen years to the birth of LORE in a dimly-lit basement in Middletown, New Jersey, we can say it was undertaken with the same wild abandon and sense of "it'll be fun!" with which Kane began editing his Inquirer.

And why can't "fun" be a motivating force? Why is "fun" looked upon by the Mr. Thatchers of the world as something in which only children should indulge? We are reminded too often of how little time we have . . . shouldn't we try to have as much fun as possible while we're here?

And boy, did we have fun with LORE.

In total, we published nine issues of what we now call LORE 1.0. Within those pages we were proud to feature work from some of our favorite writers and artists, like Harlan Ellison and Richard Corben. We were also thrilled to publish work from people who would become new friends, like Jeffrey Thomas, Dan Clore, Robert M. Price, Peter Cannon, Wayne Miller, Brian McNaughton and many others. The contents of those nine original issues earned a Deathrealm Award for Best Magazine and the Dragon's Breath Small Press Award for Best New Magazine. Harlan

Ellison's "Chatting With Anubis" went on to win The Bram Stoker Award for Best Fiction: Short Form, and The Deathrealm Award for Best Short Story, and many of the tales we published in LORE went on to receive Honorable Mentions in *Datlow and Windling's Year's Best Fantasy and Horror.* We were thrilled!

Despite our success, LORE was officially entombed in 2000 due to various pressures from that old killjoy Real Life. But the vault wasn't sealed as tightly as we thought.

This past January, 2011, we were two thousand miles, a dozen years, and worlds away from where we had first cobbled together LORE, in its first iteration. "Let's get together in Tempe for MythosCon! It'll be fun!" we said.

There's that line again.

We toyed with the idea of doing something further in the realm of weird publishing in the dozen or so years since we wedged the vault doors closed on LORE, but it started to dawn on us as we sat together over lunch in The Caffe Boa on South Mill Street on a beautiful January day that maybe we should revisit the tomb, clear the cobwebs, pull out the stake, and see what happens. And what better venue: a convention celebrating the life and works of H.P. Lovecraft (pbuh), a spiritual instigator behind LORE's halcyon adventurism.

So much has changed since the nineties. We lost a dear friend in Brian McNaughton, who shuffled off this mortal coil in May of 2004. He became a regular fixture in our exploits. We travelled frequently together to places like New York City for one of ST Joshi's Kalem Club meetings or to Providence for NecronomiCon, or to Bloomfield, NJ, to get together with Robert M. Price for one of his Esoteric Order of Dagon meetings (with folks like Joe Pulver and Mike Cisco). Other times we would simply hang out at Brian's pad, get drunk and watch monster movies. He even served as an Associate Editor of LORE under the *nom de guerre* Ricardo Santagata. Ha! Father Ric. Grand times! We miss him dearly.

Yet some things have not changed over these many years. Namely, our enthusiastic love for fantastic fiction burns as brightly as ever. This collection will serve as our introduction to the new readership that has emerged over the course of the last twelve years. We were quite something, and the tales contained herein will bear this out. The stories we've selected to appear in this volume will serve as deft ambassadors for the work we intend to start publishing again through the months to come.

"The Challenge From Below" is an homage to a round robin tale titled "The Challenge From Beyond," which appeared in the pages of *Fantasy Magazine* in 1935. H.P. Lovecraft, Robert E. Howard, A. Merritt, C.L. Moore and Frank Belknap Long created the original Challenge, and we think we provide a great answer here with our Challenge, penned by none other than Robert M. Price, Peter Cannon, Donald R. Burleson and Brian McNaughton. It was an exceedingly fulfilling project to watch develop, and we are pleased to let it loose, in its entirety, upon the public here again.

Of course, everyone knows you should never throw anything away because you never know when you might need it. Special thanks to Wayne Miller, whose illustration graces the cover of this volume, for taking that old adage to heart. Wayne's piece was originally created for the never-released LORE 10, the contents of which have since scattered to the far corners of the publishing world.

After publishing so many tales of terror, you'd think we'd have realized sooner that LORE, although laid to rest eleven years ago, could, at any moment, rise from its grave bigger, badder, and more alive than ever! We had only to say the proper words: "We should start up LORE again . . . it'll be fun."

The new series, called LORE 2.0 in-house, is being assembled as you read this. Our scope has been expanded to include more science-fiction and fantasy in addition to the horror tales we love. Be sure to join LORE in its new incarnation. It'll be . . . well, you know.

LORE is dead. Long live LORE.

Rod Heather and Sean O'Leary
October, 2011

INNARDS

Charnel Knowledge ix
Rod Heather and Sean O'Leary

CHATTING WITH ANUBIS 17
Harlan Ellison®

VISION 25
Brian McNaughton

THE GAME OF KINGS 28
Tim Emswiler

THE MANDALA 39
Kendall Evans

THE GUIDE 55
Richard Lee Byers

RAT FAMILIAR 61
Patricia Russo

EMPATHY 72
Jeffrey Thomas

THE VEHICLE 83
Brian Lumley

THANKS.. 102
Elizabeth Massie

THE GALVANIC 105
James S. Dorr

SHEETS 116
Donald R. Burleson

WATER AND THE SPIRIT... 125
Brian McNaughton

THE UNKNOWN ELIXIR 136
Dan Clore

RILE FOUTS AND DEAD JAKE SORREL 142
Lawrence Barker

THE CHALLENGE FROM BELOW
    Part One: Under the Mound 155
    Robert M. Price

    Part Two: The Trial 168
    Peter Cannon

    Part Three: The Horror at the Lake 179
    Donald R. Burleson

    Part Four: Beyond the Wall of Time 188
    Brian McNaughton

a quaint and curious volume of selected stories

CHATTING WITH ANUBIS
Harlan Ellison®

WHEN THE CORE DRILLING WAS HALTED at a depth of exactly 804.5 meters, one half mile down, Amy Guiterman and I conspired to grab Immortality by the throat and shake it till it noticed us.

My name is Wang Zicai. Ordinarily, the family name Wang—which is pronounced with the "a" in *father*, almost as if it were Wong—means "king." In my case, it means something else; it means "rushing headlong." How appropriate. Don't tell me clairvoyance doesn't run in my family . . . Zicai means "suicide." Half a mile down, beneath the blank Sahara, in a hidden valley that holds cupped in its eternal serenity the lake of the Oasis of Siwa, I and a young woman equally as young and reckless as myself, Amy Guiterman of New York City, conspired to do a thing that would certainly cause our disgrace, if not our separate deaths.

I am writing this in Yin.

It is the lost ancestral language of the Chinese people. It was a language written between the 18th and 12th centuries before the common era. It is not only ancient, it is impossible to translate. There are only five people

17

alive today, as I write this, who can translate this manuscript, written in the language of the Yin Dynasty that blossomed northeast along the Yellow River in a time long before the son of a carpenter is alleged to have fed multitudes with loaves and fishes, to have walked on water, to have raised the dead. I am no "rice christian." You cannot give me a meal and find me scurrying to your god. I am Buddhist, as my family has been for centuries. That I can write in Yin—which is to modern Chinese as classical Latin is to vineyard Italian—is a conundrum I choose not to answer in this document. Let he or she who one day unearths this text unscramble the oddities of chance and experience that brought me, "rushing headlong toward suicide," to this place half a mile beneath the Oasis of Siwa.

A blind thrust-fault, hitherto unrecorded, beneath the Mountain of the Moon, had produced a cataclysmic 7.5 temblor. It had leveled villages as far away as Bir Bū Kūsā and Abu Simbel. The aerial and satellite reconnaissance from the Gulf of Sidra to the Red Sea, from the Libyan Plateau to the Sudan, showed great fissures, herniated valleys, upthrust structures, a new world lost to human sight for thousands of years. An international team of paleoseismologists was assembled, and I was called from the Great Boneyard of the Gobi by my superiors at the Mongolian Academy of Sciences at Ulan Bator to leave my triceratops and fly to the middle of hell on earth, the great sand ocean of the Sahara, to assist in excavating and analyzing what some said would be the discovery of the age.

Some said it was the mythical Shrine of Ammon.

Some said it was the Temple of the Oracle.

Alexander the Great, at the very pinnacle of his fame, was told of the Temple, and of the all-knowing Oracle who sat there. And so he came, from the shore of Egypt down into the deep Sahara, seeking the Oracle. It is recorded: his expedition was lost, wandering hopelessly, without water and without hope. Then crows came to lead them down through the Mountain of the Moon, down to a hidden valley without name, to the lake of the Oasis of Siwa, and at its center . . . the temple, the Shrine of Ammon. It was so recorded. And one thing more. In a small and dark chamber roofed with palm logs, the Egyptian priests told Alexander a thing that affected him for the rest of his life. It is not recorded what he was told. And never again, we have always been led to believe, has the Shrine of Ammon been seen by civilized man or civilized woman.

Now, Amy Guiterman and I, she from the Brooklyn Museum and I an honored graduate of Beijing University, together we had followed Alexander's route from Paraetonium to Siwa to here, hundreds of kilometers beyond human thought or action, half a mile down, where the gigantic claw diggers had ceased their abrading, the two of us with simple pick and shovel, standing on the last thin layer of compacted dirt and rock that roofed whatever great shadowy structure lay beneath us, a shadow picked up by the most advanced deep-resonance-response readings, verified on-site by proton free-precession magnetometry and ground-penetrating radar brought in from the Sandia National Laboratory in Albuquerque, New Mexico, in the United States.

Something large lay just beneath our feet.

And tomorrow, at sunrise, the team would assemble to break through and share the discovery, whatever it might be.

But I had had knowledge of Amy Guiterman's body, and she was as reckless as I, rushing headlong toward suicide, and in a moment of foolishness, a moment that should have passed but did not, we sneaked out of camp and went to the site and lowered ourselves, taking with us nylon rope and crampons, powerful electric torches and small recording devices, trowel and whisk broom, cameras and carabiners. A pick and a shovel. I offer no excuse. We were young, we were reckless, we were smitten with each other, and we behaved like naughty children. What happened should not have happened.

·   ·   ·

We broke through the final alluvial layer and swept out the broken pieces. We stood atop a ceiling of fitted stones, basalt or even marble, I could not tell immediately. I knew they were not granite, that much I did know. There were seams. Using the pick, I prised loose the ancient and concretized mortar. It went much more quickly and easily than I would have thought, but then, I'm used to digging for bones, not for buildings. I managed to chock the large set-stone in place with wooden wedges, until I had guttered the perimeter fully. Then, inching the toe of the pick into the fissure, I began levering the stone up, sliding the wedges deeper to keep the huge block from slipping back. And finally, though the block was at least sixty or seventy centimeters thick, we were able to tilt it up and, bracing our backs against the opposite side of the hole we had dug at the bottom of the core pit, we were able to use our strong young legs to force it back and away, beyond the balance point; and it fell away with a crash.

A great wind escaped the aperture that had housed the stone. A great wind that twisted up from below in a dark swirl that we could actually see. Amy Guiterman gave a little sound of fear and startlement. So did I. Then she said, "They would have used great amounts of charcoal to set these limestone blocks in place," and I learned from her that they were not marble, neither were they basalt.

We showed each other our bravery by dangling our feet through the opening, sitting at the edge and leaning over to catch the wind. It smelled *sweet*. Not a smell I had ever known before. But certainly not stagnant. Not corrupt. Sweet as a washed face, sweet as chilled fruit. Then we lit our torches and swept the beams below.

We sat just above the ceiling of a great chamber. Neither pyramid nor mausoleum, it seemed to be an immense hall filled with enormous statues of pharaohs and beast-headed gods and creatures with neither animal nor human shape . . . and all of these statues gigantic. Perhaps one hundred times life-size.

Directly beneath us was the noble head of a time-lost ruler, wearing the *nemes* headdress and the royal ritual beard. Where our digging had dropped shards of rock, the shining yellow surface of the statue had been chipped, and a darker material showed through. "Diorite," Amy Guiterman said. "Covered with gold. Pure gold. Lapis lazuli, turquoise, garnets, rubies—the headdress is made of thousands of gems, all precisely cut . . . do you see?"

But I was lowering myself. Having cinched my climbing rope around the excised block, I was already shinnying down the cord to stand on the first ledge I could manage, the empty place between the placid hands of the pharaoh that lay on the golden knees. I heard Amy Guiterman scrambling down behind and above me.

Then the wind rose again, suddenly, shrieking up and around me like a monsoon, and the rope was ripped from my hands, and my torch was blown away, and I was thrown back and something sharp caught at the back of my shirt and I wrenched forward to fall on my stomach and I felt the cold of that wind on my bare back. And everything was dark.

Then I felt cold hands on me. All over me. Reaching, touching, probing me, as if I were a cut of sliced meat lying on a counter. Above me I heard Amy Guiterman shrieking. I felt the halves of my ripped shirt torn from my body, and then my kerchief, and then my boots, and then my stockings, and then my watch and glasses.

I struggled to my feet and took a position, ready to make an empassing or killing strike. I was no cinema action hero, but whatever was there plucking at me would have to take my life despite I fought for it!

Then, from below, light began to rise. Great light, the brightest light I've ever seen, like a shimmering fog. And as it rose, I could see that the mist that filled the great chamber beneath us was trying to reach us, to touch us, to feel us with hands of ephemeral chilling ghastliness. Dead hands. Hands of beings and men who might never have been or who, having been, were denied their lives. They reached, they sought, they implored.

And rising from the mist, with a howl, Anubis.

God of the dead, jackal-headed conductor of souls. Opener of the road to the afterlife. Embalmer of Osiris, Lord of the mummy wrappings, ruler of the dark passageways, watcher at the neverending funeral. Anubis came, and we were left, suddenly ashamed and alone, the American girl and I, who had acted rashly as do all those who flee toward their own destruction.

But he did not kill us, did not take us. How could he . . . am I not writing this for some never-to-be-known reader to find? He roared yet again, and the hands of the seekers drew back, reluctantly, like whipped curs into kennels, and there in the soft golden light reflected from the icon of a pharaoh dead and gone so long that no memory exists even of his name, there in the space half a mile down, the great god Anubis spoke to us.

At first, he thought we were "the great conqueror" come again. No, I told him, not Alexander. And the great god laughed with a terrible thin laugh that brought to mind paper cuts and the slicing of eyeballs. No, of course not that one, said the great god, for did I not reveal to him the great secret? Why should he ever return? Why should he not flee as fast as his great army could carry him, and never return? And Anubis laughed.

I was young and I was foolish, and I asked the jackal-headed god to tell *me* the great secret. If I was to perish here, at least I could carry to the afterlife a great wisdom.

Anubis looked through me.

Do you know why I guard this tomb?

I said I did not know, but that perhaps it was to protect the wisdom of the Oracle, to keep hidden the great secret of the Shrine of Ammon that had been given to Alexander.

And Anubis laughed the more. Vicious laughter that made me wish I had never grown skin or taken air into my lungs.

This is not the Shrine of Ammon, he said. Later they may have said it was, but this is what it has always been, the tomb of the Most Accursed One. The Defiler. The Nemesis. The Killer of the dream that lasted twice six thousand years. I guard this tomb to deny him entrance to the afterlife.

And I guard it to pass on the great secret.

"Then you don't plan to kill us?" I asked. Behind me I heard Amy Guiterman snort with disbelief that I, a graduate of Beijing University, could ask such an imbecile question. Anubis looked through me again, and said no, I don't have to do that. It is not my job. And then, with no prompting at all, he told me, and he told Amy Guiterman from the Brooklyn Museum, he told us the great secret that had lain beneath the sands since the days of Alexander. And then he told us whose tomb it was. And then he vanished into the mist. And then we climbed back out, hand over hand, because our ropes were gone, and my clothes were gone, and Amy Guiterman's pack and supplies were gone, but we still had our lives.

At least for the moment.

I write this now, in Yin, and I set down the great secret in its every particular. All parts of it, and the three colors, and the special names, and the pacing. It's all here, for whoever finds it, because the tomb is gone again. Temblor or jackal-god, I cannot say. But if today, as opposed to last night, you seek that shadow beneath the sand, you will find emptiness.

Now we go our separate ways, Amy Guiterman and I. She to her destiny, and I to mine. It will not be long in finding us. At the height of his power, soon after visiting the Temple of the Oracle, where he was told something that affected him for the rest of his life, Alexander the Great died of a mosquito bite. It is said. Alexander the Great died of an overdose of drink and debauchery. It is said. Alexander the Great died of murder, he was poisoned. It is said. Alexander the Great died of a prolonged, nameless fever; of pneumonia; of typhus; of septicemia; of typhoid; of eating off tin plates; of malaria. It is said. Alexander was a bold and energetic king at the peak of his powers, it is written, but during his last months in Babylon, for no reason anyone has ever been able to explain satisfactorily, he took to heavy drinking and nightly debauches . . . and then the fever came for him.

A mosquito. It is said.

No one will bother to say what has taken me. Or Amy Guiterman. We are insignificant. But we know the great secret.

Anubis likes to chat. The jackal-headed one has no secrets he chooses to keep. He'll tell it all. Secrecy is not his job. Revenge is his job. Anubis guards the tomb, and eon by eon makes revenge for his fellow gods.

The tomb is the final resting place of the one who killed the gods. When belief in the gods vanishes, when the worshippers of the gods turn away their faces, then the gods themselves vanish. Like the mist that climbs and implores, they go. And the one who lies encrypted there, guarded by the lord of the funeral, is the one who brought the world to forget Isis and Osiris and Horus and Anubis. He is the one who opened the sea, and the one who wandered in the desert. He is the one who went to the mountaintop, and he is the one who brought back the word of yet another god. He is Moses, and for Anubis revenge is not only sweet, it is everlasting. Moses—denied both Heaven and Hell—will never rest in the afterlife. Revenge without pity has doomed him to eternal exlusion, buried in the sepulcher of the gods he killed.

I sink this now, in an unmarked meter of dirt, at a respectable depth; and I go my way, bearing the great secret, no longer needing to "rush headlong," as I have already committed what suicide is necessary. I go my way, for however long I have, leaving only this warning for anyone who may yet seek the lost Shrine of Ammon. In the words of Amy Guiterman of New York City, spoken to a jackal-headed deity, "I've got to tell you, Anubis, you are one *tough* grader." She was not smiling when she said it.

VISION
Brian McNaughton

AFTER DON DIEGO SHOT THE INDIAN, he rearmed his crossbow and passed it to me.

"Keep your eyes on these cattle," he said.

No order should have been easier to follow, given such "cattle" as the cacique's women, wearing only the skimpy aprons that satisfied their undemanding notion of modesty, but Don Diego distracted me by gouging out our victim's eyes.

At last obeying the order, I was horrified to be greeted by smiles. I couldn't begin to imagine what they were thinking. I would never forget the sight of the caponized boys they fattened in cages for feasts. Perhaps they viewed the murder and mutilation of their lord as jolly sport.

"See?" Don Diego held out the eyes on his palm.

As we had been told, they were not human eyes at all, but gemstones.

"What do you suppose they're worth?" I asked disingenuously.

"Worth?" he laughed. "This man had no eyes, but he saw better than any cat or eagle. He saw through walls, even through the walls that separate us from heaven and hell. What is it worth to be king? To be pope? To be God?"

I crossed myself. "He was a king, yes, of a pimple on the world's backside."

"Only, dear Ricardo, because he lacked imagination, daring and ruthlessness. Since when have these ever been Castilian deficiencies? Now you must do what we spoke of."

"I cannot."

He smiled the very smile I had expected . . . "This is why I am a captain, and you are not. I know your weaknesses, and you shall be my foremost servant when I rule the world. Take these now, and guard them."

Though he lacked true imagination, Don Diego's daring and ruthlessness had no like, He took a deep breath and pressed his thumbs to his own eyes. In one, deci sive stroke he gouged them out. Only a suppressed sob marked the pain that even I felt as I watched.

"The stones," he hissed between clenched teeth. "Quickly!"

"Imagination, ruthlessness and daring are futile, my captain," I said, "when they are diluted by trust."

I raised the crossbow and shot him. The women giggled as the show vaulted beyond even savage expectations.

Patting bare rumps at random, I strode onto the beach to feast my eyes on a vast sea displaying ten distinct shades of green, with at least ten more discernible in the conical islands that wandered off to the kingdom of the clouds. Directly before me, I focused on the face of the cacique's loveliest wife. In no one place had I seen so much evidence of God's grandeur, and I assured the Blessed Virgin that I had no designs whatever on His prerogatives.

My gallant captain had set the standard to which I must rise, and I did.

The pain—I would describe it, but it was blotted out by the agony in my manly parts as a dainty knee, driven by primitive strength, crushed soft flesh against bone. As I fell to my knees a club tore off my helmet and perfected my paralysis. I couldn't resist when the magical gems were taken from my very hand.

Vision

Men's hands gripped me and hauled me to my feet. I was propelled through a gale of stones, sticks, sand and spit, while the taunts and jeers reached a level of noise that would have got these barbarians evicted from hell itself. Even if they could have understood my impassioned pleas and explanations, no one could have heard them. It gave me some small comfort to change my tack and tell the scoundrels I should have begun the day by crucifying every last one of them, an omission that the Admiral himself would set right.

No insult or indignity was neglected as I was stripped, then kicked into a place of confinement, where I lost consciousness.

It might have been noon or midnight when I woke, how could I know? Female voices murmured around me. Exploring by touch, I found food, ample food, and I surprised myself by eating ravenously. The Arawaks are impenetrable creatures, driven by whim and superstition. Could they not have changed their minds and decided to treat me once more as a pampered guest?

I called out, and the voices that responded seemed not at all hostile. Exploring further, I learned that I was in a wooden cage. It took almost no time at all to grasp that the soft voices came from the other cages around me, the fattening-cages of the caponized boys.

THE GAME OF KINGS
Tim Emswiler

"The chessboard is the world, the pieces are the phenomena of the universe, the rules the laws of nature. The player on the other side is hidden from us."

—Thomas Henry Huxley

OUTSIDE MY ROOM THE RAIN IS COMING DOWN IN TORRENTS, driven by a fierce wind that rattles the window in its casement, the kind of night about which the phrase *not fit for man nor beast* must have been coined. Yet this is precisely the kind of night in which Rhodes and I took such delight. Just a couple of weeks ago, such a night would have found us sitting here or in his rooms, warm and comfortable, the tranquility of our surroundings separated from the maelstrom outside only by a mere pane of glass, ourselves separated only by a chessboard.

Good God, that is just how he spoke. Rhodes was like that; he had the kind of charisma that made all around him imitate his speech and mannerisms, whether consciously or not.

But now Rhodes is gone and his chessboard, over which we spent so many hours, sits unattended in the corner of my room, covered with black cloth like a memorial.

Funny that I should use that word, memorial. I do not know that he is dead, simply that he is gone.

Perhaps it would be easier to begin at the beginning, an analyst might suggest at this point. For me, of course, it began the moment I met him.

I had been granted admission to a rather exclusive men's club, thanks to the kind offices of my brother. Even on my first visit I heard Rhodes' name mentioned, and what I heard was anything but complimentary. When I finally met the man himself, I simply attributed these remarks to the envy that sporting, athletic types tend to feel for those of a more cerebral temperament. He certainly looked the part of the scholar, with his pale complexion, thick-lensed eyeglasses and somewhat outdated style of dress. A man of such slight build looked quite out of place among the hearty members of the club; I was surprised at the strength behind his handshake when my brother introduced us.

I soon learned that Rhodes was an avid chess player, and within minutes of our meeting we were seated across the board from each other in a corner of the club's sitting room, oblivious to the chatter of those around us.

"I did not think that this club accepted anyone who was not the sportsman type," Rhodes said as he contemplated his reply to my last move. "I certainly did not think that they would accept any chess players after myself."

"Well," I replied, somewhat taken aback, "no one asked me if I played chess when I applied for membership." The room was heated oppressively by the fireplace before which several other members were gathered, drinking and smoking.

"I'm joking, of course," Rhodes muttered without looking up from the board. "Chess is not what these fellows find troubling, but the way I feel about chess."

"Certainly anyone familiar with the game would understand that there are a number of obsessives among its adherents," I said, with a smile that Rhodes did not see because he was busy removing from the board a pawn that I had foolishly left unprotected.

Abruptly, his gaze turned icy. "Perhaps you would like to tell me what you have heard about me," he said.

"Why, nothing at all," I stammered. "I simply assumed from your remarks that the other members have trouble understanding your passion for the game."

At that he laughed, loudly enough to momentarily halt the conversations buzzing around us. He did not speak until the noise had resumed.

"Indeed, my friend, they most certainly do not understand. A pity, actually. There are some bright minds here, and some of them could, given time and tutoring, become exceptional players. But there is more to the game than the playing of it, and that is what is beyond the grasp of even the most educated man here."

I was at a loss. Finally, with a self-depreciating laugh, I said, "I'm afraid that it is probably beyond me, as well. I am a poet, myself."

He regarded me with a look so piercing, so invasive, that it was all I could do to meet it. "No," he said, "I think that you have precisely the sort of mind to comprehend the ramifications of the game, those aspects which go beyond the simple movements of the pieces. A poet's mind, I think, is to one's advantage in this case."

Then, without looking down at the board, without the least change of expression, he moved a piece and said "Checkmate."

.   .   .

It would be incorrect to say that we became friends, but we did become constant companions, and opponents. Rhodes never failed to beat me, soundly and effortlessly, yet he seemed to take no satisfaction from his victories. No sooner would he announce checkmate than he would ask me to play again. And I would always agree; not out of any hope that I might defeat him, but because I suspected that Rhodes *needed* to play, and not just against anyone. Somehow I felt that he needed *me*.

As time went on, we began to talk more during our games; or, I should say, Rhodes spoke and I listened. I must admit that I found our conversations distracting and my play suffered as a result, but eventually my play ceased to matter. Being in his presence became for me the sole object of our meetings, chess simply an excuse for them. And, by some strange paradox, the less I cared about how well I played, the better I played.

"Absolute silence is not requisite for success in this game," Rhodes once said. "In fact, quite the opposite. Think about it. If you concentrate too long on one object or think too long about a certain topic, you lose your ability to focus. Lines become blurred, distinctions vague, patterns become chaos. This is diametrically opposed to the goal of chess, which is to bring order out of the chaos of the myriad possible moves that could be made."

Only on rare occasions did he speak of his *theories* about the game, usually in such abstract terms that I became more confused than I had been. The few fragments of his notebooks which survived the fire provided little in the way of further explanation.

We soon stopped going to the club altogether. I could not understand why he had ever gone there in the first place. The presence of the others seemed to inhibit him, and I found it intolerable that such a mind should be stifled.

As Rhodes' experiment (as it clearly must be called, much as I hoped that it was more) progressed, I came closer to beating him, and he began to show signs of actually enjoying our games.

One night we were in Rhodes' small apartments, which were made even more cramped by the numerous bookshelves which lined its walls and a fireplace so large as to be incongruous. Rhodes was usually reticent when questioned directly; one needed to wait for the urge to talk to strike him. But on this night my curiosity got the best of me. Perhaps the fact that he had drunk more brandy than was his custom emboldened me.

"You mystify me," I said. "You take no pleasure from winning, as far as I can tell, and your enthusiasm for the game seems to increase in direct proportion to how close you come to losing."

Rhodes smiled at this, like a teacher with a deficient student who has just succeeded in drawing an obvious conclusion, took a sip of his brandy, then spoke in the oratorical tone he always used when he was quoting the words of another. It was a little game of his, a way of testing me.

"A win always seems shallow; it is the lose that is so profound and suggests nasty infinities."

I shrugged, conceding that I did not know the quotation.

"E.M. Forster," Rhodes said. "It seems that he understood much. It was also he who said, *There are some curious features about games, moments of piercing reality when an unknown process is suddenly reflected like a star."*

"So, this is what you are after, an *unknown process* hidden within the rules of chess?"

"A process, or a source . . . perhaps a pathway, or a door." He noted my expression and impatience clouded his features. "Chess, you see, is not a science so much as it is an art. To be sure, intelligence plays a vital role. But what raises chess above the level of any other game is *vision.* Understand, I am not talking about winning the game. Winning at chess requires nothing more than study and practice. I myself am no artist, yet with all modesty I consider myself an exceptional chess player. I am talking about truly *understanding* the game, seeing beyond the surface of it, and this requires a unique mind, one that comprises equal parts intellect and artistic sensibility. A combination of my mind and yours, so to speak. My skill at chess can be had by anyone with a desire for it. But you could not teach me to see with the eyes of an artist. In order to see if my theories have any merit . . . "

At this I interrupted him. "But, what exactly are these theories of yours that you speak of so obliquely? I would not argue that chess is a game like no other, but it is, in the end, simply a game. You make it sound as if it had some kind of unfathomable significance . . . "

The intensity of his gaze brought me up short.

"Exactly," he said.

Abruptly he stood and strode across to one of the bookcases and took down a well-worn volume. The book opened practically unassisted to the page Rhodes was after, as though it had been referred to many times.

"This man, C.E.M. Joad, was on to something," Rhodes said as he stood before the blaze burning brightly in the fireplace. "More, I suspect, than he ever knew. He compares chess to mathematics, noting that both deal with combinations and relations between non-material things—although we see and touch the pieces on the chessboard, what we are actually thinking about is not the pieces but the possible combinations between them. As Joad puts it, these relations represent an order of reality different from the visible, tangible world."

As he spoke, a halo of light seemed to form around his body. Amazed, I watched as the glow wrapped itself around him, as if in a matter of moments it would consume him. With an effort I forced my eyes to focus, only then realizing that what I had seen was merely a trick of the firelight behind him, perhaps distorted by the brandy I had consumed myself. As my normal vision returned and Rhodes' figure again became distinct, it looked as if he had stepped unscathed from the mouth of a tunnel of fire.

"According to Joad," Rhodes was saying, "it is no accident that the three areas in which one finds infant prodigies are music, mathematics, and chess, because all three of these deal with this different order of reality."

Still disconcerted by my optical illusion, I found myself struggling to make sense of his words. He was pacing now, animated, and his eyes caught and held the glow of the firelight as he read from the book.

"*I like to think that one of the reasons for it may be that the soul has inhabited such an order of reality before it was incarnated in the body, and brings with it to this world a memory of the harmonies of sound and combinations of number which exist in that world, a memory which it does not immediately forget. Presently the memory is wiped out by experience of this world, and the chess or mathematical prodigy is a prodigy no longer.*"

Rhodes stopped pacing and turned on me with a look that can only be described as triumphant.

"He goes on to say that the minds of our greatest chess geniuses, like Morphy and Capablanca, are simply minds in which the memory of this other world has not faded."

Then Rhodes' face fell. "Alas, I suspect that Joad was merely being romantic when he expressed himself this way. He obviously saw that there is more to the game than is generally acknowledged, but I doubt that he took himself as seriously as he should have."

This talk, combined with the effects of the drink, had me somewhat agitated, and I made a foolish move. With a swift movement of his arm, Rhodes swept the pieces from the board and glared at me fiercely. "Perhaps," he hissed, "you will return when you are ready to play."

With that, I left his apartments, determined never to return.

♦　　♦　　♦

But of course I did. One does not simply take leave of a man like Rhodes. I stayed away for a time, but eventually I was pulled back to my seat across the board from him.

How can I explain this? Anyone who has ever been in the presence of such a man needs no explanation, and for those who have not, no explanation will suffice.

We never spoke of the period of my absence. But things had changed. Rhodes had changed.

He now played music at loud volumes during our games; Mussorgsky's *Pictures at an Exhibition* and Wagner's *Ring of the Nibelung* provided the accompaniment to his increasing mania. He explained that this was merely an extension of his earlier conclusions about silence being detrimental to one's game.

"Listen to that music!" He nearly had to shout to make himself heard above the din. "It unlocks doors in the mind, unleashes creative energies that would perish in silence and stillness!"

To my astonishment, my next move came to me without any conscious thought; I simply looked at the board and moved my knight, knowing that in three moves I would win his queen and that there was no way for him to prevent it. The look on Rhodes' face at this move was almost childlike in its glee.

"You see? I have never taught you a single thing about chess, all I have done is played against you over and over, yet you have progressed at an amazing rate. You begin to see the game as I see it." Rhodes was so excited that he stood and began to pace around the room. He paused at the window, then turned to me like a prosecutor attempting to startle a witness.

"And of course, it is raining! The wind is picking up. Do you think that is a coincidence?"

I said nothing, thinking his question a rhetorical one. Suddenly he had me by the shirtfront, his face only inches from mine. "Well, *do you*?"

"No, of course not," I replied, trying my best to sound sincere and to suppress the tremor in my voice.

Apparently satisfied, he sat back down in his chair, but made no move to resume our game.

"Did you know," Rhodes said after some minutes had passed in silence, "that it is estimated that there are more different possible chess games than there are atoms in the universe? Does it seem reasonable to assume that such a game, such an *art*, was invented by one person? The game must have started somewhere, somehow, mustn't it? But could a mortal mind have conceived of anything so complex, so infinitely variable, yet at the same time so simple that a child can master the fundamentals?"

Rhodes' eyes were focused on a distance that only he could see. "All of those possible games. And one of them, the perfect game. A game that has not yet been played. But it will be. When the right minds, the right forces, face each other across the board . . . " Now his eyes looked directly into mine as the music ended, plunging the room into a silence in which his voice was startlingly loud. " . . . it will be played."

I was making ready to leave when Rhodes detained me with a hand on my arm. "I had a dream last night," he said in a troubled voice. "In this dream, I was a spectator at a chess match at which there were no players." His hand tightened convulsively on my arm. "You have not looked into the abyss until you have seen pieces move of their own accord across the chessboard, obeying rules which you believed to be of human authorship."

This did not strike me as being at all horrible or frightful, but I said nothing.

⬧　　⬧　　⬧

I was trapped; there is no other way to say it. As much as I knew that remaining within the sphere of Rhodes' influence could bring me nothing but misfortune, I remained in his thrall. And yes, I must admit, I had begun to envision that perfect game of which he now spoke often, and to imagine myself a part of that game. The results of that game I contemplated only in dreams; dreams which I willfully drove from my mind upon waking.

Yet, I was wrong. If this game took place, it did so without my participation.

The other tenants in Rhodes' building noticed nothing out of the ordinary that night, save for the fact that the music of Wagner was playing at louder volume than usual, loud enough to be heard over the storm which battered the building throughout the night. No one was seen entering or leaving Rhodes' rooms.

The following day, investigators could find no evidence to help them determine the source of the fire, nor its bizarre nature; bizarre in that the fire consumed nearly everything within Rhodes' apartments, yet left the rest of the building completely untouched.

Of the dream which I had while the storm and the fire raged, I can remember nothing. But I know that I did dream.

Perhaps Rhodes had found another opponent to fill the hours during which I was absent. Perhaps, however, he was alone that night. In any case, a game of chess was played.

When his landlady allowed me to enter his rooms, I found myself standing in the midst of ashes and blackened walls; all of the furnishings had burned so completely as to leave no trace of their existence. All, that is, but the mahogany table with its inlaid marble chessboard, upon which the wooden pieces, unharmed by the fire, were arranged as in a game still in progress.

The last thing I had done before taking my leave of Rhodes the previous night was to return the pieces to their starting positions after our last game had been completed.

Beneath the table, caught under one of the legs, I found some pieces of paper, charred but still legible, covered with Rhodes' meticulous and compact handwriting. I conducted a thorough search, but if any more pages had endured the blaze, they had been taken by the investigators who had preceded me.

These same investigators, despite an exhaustive search, had found no human remains among the ashes. No fragments of bone or teeth, nothing which would normally survive even the most intense flames.

A game was played, or at least begun, and it appears that it did not matter that Rhodes was not the artistic type. I fear that it will not matter that I am.

I brought the board to my room, careful (for reasons I cannot explain) not to disturb the position of the pieces. I told myself that the black cloth was in Rhodes' honor; I told myself that the sight of the chessmen did not disturb me.

I was lying to myself. As foolish as I feel putting such emotions into words, I am intimidated by these pieces of wood, small enough to fit easily into the palm of my hand. In my mind, the rook has taken on the dimensions of a massive tower, a keep from which I could never escape; the visage of the horse has undergone a hideous transformation, all blasted eyes and flaring, flaming nostrils. I can barely tolerate the thought that these pieces wait mere feet from me, hidden beneath that thin black cloth.

Yet I cannot bring myself to remove the board from my room. It is, as I said, a memorial, but it is more; it is an invitation, to Rhodes or to something else, a doorway through which I sometimes expect Rhodes' ghostly hand to emerge to begin another game.

Ghostly? But he is not dead. He is simply gone.

Again I read one of the fragments of his notes which I found among the ashes, although by now I have it committed to memory. "Chess," Rhodes wrote, "has been called *the game of kings*. But who, in fact, are the true kings? Do the players truly control the pieces, or do the pieces have some volition of their own of which we suspect nothing? Or is there something else, something which orchestrates the actions of the players as the players conduct the movements of the pieces?"

I let the paper fall to my desk and restlessly wander around the room. Against my will, my gaze falls upon the chessboard, the varying heights of the pieces creating peaks and valleys in the cloth. As I draw nearer, I become convinced that this topography has changed since I brought the board here to my room.

The pieces are in motion. The game has resumed.

THE MANDALA
Kendall Evans

He was browsing the outdoor cafes of Amsterdam seeking a likely place for lunch when he spotted her: The Girl In The Wall. It was how he thought of her, as The Girl In The Wall, the first letter of each word capitalized.

Uncertain because it had been a decade and more since their last meeting, he approached her table. A young couple eating close-by glanced up curiously as he shifted aside an empty chair that was in his way. She sat alone at a rear table, immersed in a book, her body turned oddly, half toward the restaurant's brickwork at the inner corner of the patio. A coffee and a small empty plate before her, as if she had just finished a simple continental breakfast. "Joanne?" he said; "Is it really you?"

Despite the intervening years, despite the fact that she had been a pre-adolescent when he saw her last, something about the young woman's profile convinced him he was right. He had always been excellent with faces; lousy with names. But of course he had not forgotten *her* name.

She glanced up, regarding him from one side of her face, something bird-like in the scrutiny. It took her a moment. "Dr. Bastian, isn't it?" she finally said. "Arnold Bastian?"

"Yes. My God, what a coincidence, running into you here." He wanted to question her; interrogate her. Instead, he forced himself to be polite; to make conversation. "I'm surprised you recognized me, after so many years."

"Sit down," she said. "Please. Join me." And yet she did not sound that glad to see him. "What are you up to these days, Doctor, prowling the streets of Amsterdam alone?"

He barked a short, nervous laugh—not the laugh he would choose to own, but the only one he could ever summon spontaneously. "I'm not really alone. I'm vacationing with my second wife, Barbara. A sort of delayed honeymoon. We landed at Schipolt Airport this morning, and I'm afraid she's suffering from jet lag. Kicked me out of our room and told me to find something to eat while she catches up on her beauty rest. What about you?"

"I'm traveling with my sister."

The sister. Dana Collier. He had forgotten her completely. She had been—what?—two years younger than Joanne.

"I barely met your sister. I did speak with your mother, however . . . several times. How is she?"

Joanne shrugged. "She's fine. I'm not living at home now, but we keep in touch."

"I see," he said, preoccupied. He did not—could not—allow the amenities to go on any longer. Unresolved curiosity that had stayed with him all these years, rankling, compelled him to say: "Do you mind if I ask you some questions, Joanne? About what happened to you?"

"No. No, I don't mind. Go ahead."

"During our sessions," he said, trying not to sound too blunt, "You did a good job of describing your experiences, considering your age—even though it didn't fully explain what occurred. You've had a long time to think about it. Have you remembered anything at all you didn't mention before? Anything relevant?"

"No . . . no, but I'm better at expressing what happened. What I saw. That circle . . . I said it looked like a doily, but it didn't really. Some of the designs in it were pictographic, representations of birds and dog-like creatures. Most looked like letters in a foreign language, an unfamiliar alphabet. Greek, maybe; I can't be sure. After it started turning, the symbols all blurred together. But, God, I'll never forget that glowing form, hovering in mid-air, spinning. If I had to name it now, I'd say 'Mandala.'"

"A mandala," he answered dryly. "Yes. I thought of that."

Beyond the tables, pigeons alternately strutted and darted for scraps. He watched them, gathering his thoughts. Passers-by startled several into flight, but a moment later they returned. Two beaks descended at nearly the same instant upon a single ragged crust of pastry; it catapulted away from both birds. Upon the throat of one, a subtle rainbow of colors, luminous regardless of the low morning cloud cover.

"While I was counseling you . . . questioning you . . . I went back and re-read Carl Jung, and especially everything he had to say about mandalas as symbols of psychic unity. Not that it helped at all."

"Tell me something," Joanne said coldly, a challenge: "Did you ever really believe me?"

♦   ♦   ♦

At the time of the incident he had been a police psychiatrist, had not yet broken away to form his own private practice. He still remembered the sunlight spilling through the windshield, the empty cage of the back seat, the grained stock of the mounted rifle, and the new vehicle smell of the patrolcar. The patrolman himself he did not remember so well, save that he was very young. Time had reduced him to anonymity, a sort of generic rookie. Arn had just turned thirty, and the officer seemed like a high school student.

He was seldom called to the scene. Usually he counseled police involved in shootings, or abused children brought down to the station; questioned them, to find out what they had been subjected to. But once he'd tried to talk a despondent youth on a freeway overpass out of jumping, and once he'd talked by phone, from an adjacent building, to a gunman with hostages. He'd assumed, when he climbed into the patrolcar, that this was a similar incident—and the officer proved equally uninformed.

They halted abruptly before a sprawling house in Bel Aire. An ambulance, a fire truck, and several other police cars were already present: spinning/flashing emergency lights, diminished by late afternoon sunshine. Several reporters clustered outside, restrained from access to the premises by a makeshift barrier. He wondered how they had arrived so promptly— who had tipped them off? And what the hell was going on here, anyway? Neighbors gathered on lawns, on the walk, talking, looking this way.

Sergeant Michaelson met him on the curb. "We're trying to keep the girl calm. Keep her from squirming around too much and hurting herself." Apparently the other believed he had already been briefed.

Turning before Arn had a chance to frame questions, the sergeant led him inside.

For a moment he saw without seeing, unable to absorb the stark image of a young girl stuck halfway inside a wall. As if the wall had temporarily lost its solidity while she attempted to pass through it, and re-solidified too soon. Or as if the wall had been constructed around her. Both explanations made equal sense. Equal nonsense.

He felt overwhelmed. There seemed to be too many people in the room, police and firemen and family members, a plain-clothes detective he recognized; still others he could not place at all. Shaking it off, he forced himself to be professional.

"What's the girl's name?" he asked.

"Joanne," the sergeant answered. "Joanne Collier."

It was apparent that the girl could neither move nor talk. Her mouth was partially open and a section of the wall actually extended beyond her parted lips and teeth. He guessed her to be about nine years old. There was something nearly bovine in the way her one visible eye rolled with panic. The wall nearly bisected the very center of her face.

Arn approached slowly, halting—because he was a stranger to her—just a little beyond normal conversational range.

"Hello, Joanne," he said gently.

She made an odd, grunting sound. He surmised that even her vocal cords were restricted. Obvious why they did not want her thrashing about—with the wall constricting her so tightly, it might be possible to strain muscles or dislocate a joint by trying to wrench free. Merely breathing and getting enough air must be difficult.

"Don't try to talk, Joanne. I know it might take a little while, but we're going to get you out of there."

An attractive woman in her mid-forties, well-dressed, held Joanne's hand. Her mother? The family resemblance was obvious, both blondes, and the one eyebrow of Joanne's that he could see, like the woman's, so pale it seemed to disappear. They shared a Nordic look, despite dark California tans. He knew that the mother's presence and touch accomplished more than he could have hoped to achieve. At the same time, it wouldn't hurt to offer a few soothing words.

"There's a little game we can play to help beat the time, Joanne. To make it pass more quickly. I want you to imagine that you're not here at all, but somewhere else—a very pleasant place, a sunny clearing in the woods, a natural picnic-spot between stately trees. There's a stream murmuring nearby, and your mother is there with you."—The mother glanced at him; her expression seemed to acknowledge the rightness of his words.

"Your mother is with you, holding your hand, and you feel so content that you don't want to move at all . . . " He kept his voice mellow; hypnotic. Helping the girl to establish her own light trance of beta rhythms. "Content to let the time drift by; there's no reason to hurry your thoughts. No reason to worry about—"

Sergeant Michaelson touched his shoulder. "Come with me a moment," he said quietly. "I want to show you something."

Michaelson was a boozy veteran, in Arn Bastian's experience as competent a professional as one could hope for, no matter the years of hard drinking and the complexion that showed it. On duty—even past the midnight hours of an extended shift—Michaelson was always trim, alert, and well-groomed. Always in control.

He led Arn from the room, along a short length of hall, and then into a bedroom that shared one wall with the dining area they had just departed.

Down low, a shoe was visible. An ankle, and a small section of the girl's calf.

Higher up, a seemingly disembodied arm. It had a mannequin-like look to it, but only because of the way it was situated, protruding from the wall as if mounted, an absurd or surrealistic trophy. An instant later the small hand clenched itself into a fist as if with pain, and the mannequin-illusion vanished.

He thought of taking hold of the hand to offer comfort, but realized that it might come as a shock to the girl, since she could not see him. As if she had reached through into another world, and touched something alien.

"How the hell did it happen?" he asked, now that they were alone. "How *could* it happen?"

"We don't know anything yet," Michaelson admitted. "Hopefully the girl can give us some answers once we get her out."

"Have you ever seen anything like this before?" he asked, knowing mid-way that it was a stupid question.

"Are you kidding?" Michaelson said angrily. "This is fucking impossible, is what *this* is."

"What do you plan, exactly?"

Michaelson shrugged. "The contractor we called in wants to take it slow. Open up one layer of plaster—in the other room first, leave this side intact—get a look inside the wall to see exactly what needs doing to free her."

"Is she in pain?"

"Her mother worked out some signals before you arrived. The girl squeezes her mother's hand once for 'yes', and twice for 'no'. She says she's all right. Of course there could be internal injuries, or a wound that we can't see because of the wall . . . we have no way of knowing yet. The physician . . . he's the tall one, with a stoop . . . says her blood pressure's elevated. And her pulse."

He felt he was missing something. He glanced around the room, as if he might find it there.

"Is this her room?"

"I'm not sure. She has a younger sister. It might belong to either. I'll check if it's important."

"No." Suddenly the elusive thought surfaced. "Where's the father?"

"He's on his way over right now."

"Have one of your officers meet him outside when he arrives, to explain about his daughter, and minimize the possibility of any danger. Make sure he won't panic when he sees Joanne. I don't want him frightening her. Something else . . . "

"What's that?" Michaelson's other plus was that he listened, with an open mind, to what Arn had to say. Infrequently he disagreed, but not without thinking it through.

"I want to tell the girl what we're doing every step of the way. Ask her, each step, if she's ready for us to begin. It'll give her a sense of control over the situation. Lord knows that's something she doesn't have very much of right now. And Michaelson?"

"Yes?"

"Do you think there's any chance this whole thing is a hoax?"

The other hesitated. "The possibility occurred to me. My instincts tell me no."

In the living room, portable lights had been set up. Insulated cables ran through a doorway. He realized the power in this part of the house must have been shut down.

Disbelief the predominant expression on faces all about him.

A blanket had been stapled to the wall to shield the girl from flying bits of plaster. After Arn spoke briefly with Joanne, one of the contractors went to work with a portable power saw. Plaster dust spurted liquidly away from the nearly invisible blur of spinning saw teeth.

Talk became impossible; the noise of the saw was horrendous. The girl closed her eye, as if wincing away from the sensation. He wondered about vibrations. The saw's operator paused every few minutes, removing sections of plaster, allowing the roomful of people—and the girl herself—a moment of quiet. The quiet had its own impact in the wake of raucous grinding that seemed to sandpaper his brain.

Eventually the majority of the plaster surrounding the child had been removed. Seeing the interior of the wall illustrated her predicament even more vividly. One of the wooden vertical beams rested atop her head and appeared to pass right through her. The contractor, spikes of curly-red hair jutting out beneath his cap, gripped the beam and ran his saw through it about half a foot above her head. Afterwards, the length of wood pulled free with little resistance. Gesturing his intent, Arn took it from the other's hand and turned it, examining the surface which had rested against Joanne's head. It bore a precise, dimensional image of her hair; the lines of individual strands clearly visible.

Michaelson, looking over his shoulder, grunted. "Just like a goddamn fossil," he said, shaking his head in disbelief.

The rescue efforts continued. He glanced at his watch, astonished to realize that more than ninety minutes had passed since his arrival. Plaster dust filled the air, prickling his sinuses—but it was someone behind him who sneezed. One of the workers accidentally bumped against him; he blinked his eyes, looked at Joanne...and the impossibility of the wall's embrace struck him once again, full force.

And what, Arn wondered, had become of the part of the wall that had formerly occupied the space now occupied by her body? Where had its molecules, its jittering atoms and spinning electrons, been exiled to?

Once Joanne's head was free, only the section of plaster partially in her mouth remaining, the doctor—tall and slump-shouldered, he fit Michaelson's description—moved in close and said, "Open wide," as if about to apply a tongue depressor during a routing physical exam—but his voice shook slightly, and so did his hand. With exaggerated care he turned the puzzle-piece of plaster horizontally, so that the width of her mouth would accommodate its passage, and slowly tugged it free.

"It was *chok*ing me," Joanne said—her first words. And not with fear or pain, he thought, but with relief. And for the first time he felt confident that she would be okay.

· · ·

His no-doubt red eyes felt sensitive to the light on the drive over to the Collier residence the following day. He was all on edge, sharply alert despite the fatigue of a nearly sleepless night. An unusual bout of insomnia that was easily explained; he had been too keyed up by the day's fantastic events to relax properly. And anticipation of the upcoming interview with Joanne that her mother had reluctantly granted him—he had referred to it as a counseling and de-briefing session to persuade her—added to his restlessness.

Anita Collier greeted him at the door with a reserved smile and led him to the dining room, where Joanne sat with her back to the offending wall. A large panel of plywood temporarily covered the missing plaster, as innocent-looking as a boarded-up broken window. The choice of this room for the interview surprised him, but he said nothing of it.

"Hello, Joanne. I understand they've given you some tests at the hospital."

"Yes," she answered. "The doctors don't have all the results yet, but they think I'm fine. Fit as a fiddle, Dr. Chandler said." She grinned at the cliché.

"Dr. Chandler. Is he the one who took the piece of plaster out of your mouth?"

"Yes."

Difficult to reconcile the girl before him with the child he had watched being rescued. Looking slightly nervous but still self-possessed, she wore a summer dress with a yellow floral pattern, her hair neatly swept back into a pony tail. Previously he had guessed her age as eight or nine, but he knew she was actually eleven years old, and today he perceived a level of maturity that fear and stress had temporarily erased.

After setting up his portable Sony, he urged Joanne to tell him about the day before. Smoke-colored plastic panels obscured the tape reels. He looked close to confirm their turning.

"But I don't understand what happened," she said. "I don't understand any of it." She looked stubborn; frightened by her memories. He wondered whether his own urgency might be contributing to her fear and thickened his mask of calm.

"That doesn't matter. You can still tell me what you saw. And what you felt. What time did it happen, Joanne?"

She shrugged. "I'm not sure. Three-thirty, maybe."

"After school?"

"Yes."

Her voice was soft; reluctant. He turned the recorder's volume up to compensate.

"What school do you attend?"

"Madison."

"An elementary school? And you're in the...what grade?"

"Sixth."

One word responses. He had to get her talking; believed that he was on the verge of genuine insight. "Begin with your walk home, Joanne. Tell me about that."

Her eyes looked distant; disturbed. As if memory allowed her to re-live the experience. He listened carefully, making himself receptive, attempting to live it with her in his imagination.

The walk along a residential street, accompanied part way by a friend named Shawna. Arriving home, surprised to find the house empty. A note on the door. From her mother.

Dr. Arnold Bastian: Your mother was usually home in the afternoons? Joanne Collier: Yes, but not yesterday. The note said she was shopping.

When I unlocked the door there was mail on the floor. I picked it up. One of the packages was a book.

A.B.: How did you know it was a book?

J.C.: It was a flat box, shaped like a book. It said the name of a book club, printed on it.

A.B.: Go on, Joanne. What happened next?

J.C.: I opened the box. Then I opened the book, to look at the pictures inside.

A.B.: (prompting) What pictures?

J.C.: Pictures of the Indians. Their tools and costumes...I mean, not costumes, the clothes they wore. About halfway through the book there was a picture of a circle, with designs in it. Like a doily. It filled the whole page.

Wearing a vague expression, Joanne let her voice trail away. Just as he prepared a verbal nudge, she continued. "It was . . . weird. The . . . circle. I kept staring at it. And then it started to turn. The book didn't move, it was just the picture turning, all by itself. Slow at first, but then faster and faster. It was glowing, too, filled with rainbow colors, but brighter and brighter, and spinning around and around. It lifted up off the page and stood up, it wasn't flat anymore. It was just hanging there, in the middle of the air, like magic. It got bigger and bigger. Taller than my mother. When it moved over to the wall I followed it. It was like being in a dream. I . . . was going somewhere. I was going to a place where everything is pretty and perfect and nothing ever dies. All I had to do was step through the circle."

Her voice altered; became that of a lost child. "It was like . . . like sleep walking. When I was little, I remember, sometimes I walked in my sleep and woke up in the kitchen. I was nearly there, I could see the tower made out of crystal, but then I heard my mother calling me, I heard the front door close . . . and the circle disappeared."

Enthralled, he tried to imagine the luminous spin of it, but the picture refused to form, remained mere words told to him, the impossible fabrication of an eleven-year-old. Not a satisfactory explanation at all, since it merely explained one mystery with another, and thus explained nothing.

He wanted to believe but did not want to believe, because both the event and the girl's story contradicted—totally contradicted—his conception of the world as a realm of rational cause and effect. And the calm authoritative voice of the doctor on the tape that he would later listen to again and again, as well as the flattened affect of the transcripts, belied his actual mental state at the time. He was going through a bitter divorce from Fran, due to be final in less than two weeks. He was contemplating a career change. He had witnessed events that he did not believe possible, events that might even be classified as supernatural, and he had the distinct feeling that his world was tumbling down all around him. How much more bewildering it must be for this child before him who had suffered the actual event.

"After the circle went away," she concluded, "It was like waking up, like everything that had happened was just a dream. But I really was stuck in the wall, and I couldn't get out."

"But why were you turned sideways? If you were stepping through the wall?"

"I turned when I heard my mother come in. I was going to answer her . . . " He pictured her open mouth; the intruding plaster.

And what should he make of the crystal tower, he wondered. It was like something right out of some damn children's fairy tale.

He found himself liking Joanne. He admired her courage. Admired, too, her lucid efforts to communicate that which bordered on being incommunicable.

Initially he had hoped to find evidence of fraud, a hoax perpetrated by Joanne or her family, but nothing at all pointed in that direction. rather than seeking publicity, Joanne's mother Anita had thwarted the press, minimizing the implausibility of her daughter's experience.

"Your mother told the media people—the reporters—that you were having some work done on the house. She said there was a small hole in the wall, just big enough that you thought you might be able to climb through, but you got stuck. She made it sound ordinary and not very threatening. But she admitted to me that there never was any hole. It was a lie—a sort of white lie. Do you know why she made up that story?" He asked, knowing the answer, wanting to be sure that Joanne fully understood.

"Yes. She said she did it to protect me. She said some people would think it was a religious miracle, but it wasn't because God would never leave a little girl stuck in a wall like that. And that other people would think it was something weird, like seeing flying saucers or ghosts, and they'd never stop pestering me for the rest of my life. She said she wants me to be able to lead a normal life, to be myself, just like this never happened."

Arn nodded. "I think she's right. It's probably the wisest choice. You need to get on with growing up, and not dwell too much on this."

Not until the final interview did he question her about the book.

"*The Plains Indians: Their Legends and Their Lives.* Is this the same book, Joanne?" He turned the cover toward her.

"Yes. It's the same one."

"Joanne, I've been through this book a half-dozen times. And your mother said that she looked too, and had you look with her. There's no picture of a circle with designs inside it. How do you explain that, Joanne?"

It was the only time she lost control. She started crying. "I'm not crazy," she said, her voice shrill. "I'm not crazy, I'm not!" She pounded one small fist upon the table; it seemed an imitation of an adult gesture, perhaps something she had seen her mother do in a moment of anger.

"I don't think you're crazy, Joanne," he said hurriedly. He rested his hand gently atop her fist. He did it self-consciously because, in his profession, he had to be so wary of fraudulent abuse charges. "No one thinks that. What happened to you was crazy, though, and if the events that led up to it are crazy too, I'm not at all surprised. That doesn't make you crazy. It just means something happened that none of us really comprehends."

What choice did he have, but to believe her.

◆　　　◆　　　◆

"My math skills improved," the adult Joanne informed him. "Did you know about that?"

Her words broke his connection with the past. "No" he admitted. "I didn't." He felt certain that she had not been as pleased by their chance encounter as he had been, and his initial enthusiasm had faded. He sensed withdrawal in her aloof posture, her failure to make eye contact, and she still sat in nearly the same awkward position as when he found her, turned half aside from him as if hiding from the world. This new revelation, though, rekindled his interest. He sat forward abruptly, rubbing at his tingling leg where the metal-framed chair had partially cut off circulation. "It wasn't something the doctors thought to test you for. And I certainly didn't think of it. We were looking more for . . . "

"Damage," Joanne supplied, when he faltered.

"Right. Damage. Emotional trauma or bodily harm. When did this sudden talent for numbers make itself known?"

"All those medical tests." She shook her head slightly. "It wasn't until later in the school year, when they gave us the M.A.T. tests. All my other scores were on a par with previous years, but my math results went nearly off the scale. It's something that's stayed with me. I'm in the mathematical physics program at Cambridge now, on a scholarship. Stephen Hawking has been reviewing some of my work. They seem to think I'm . . . promising."

For a moment the name didn't click, and then he recalled a television special on PBS, Stephen Hawking in his wheelchair, a victim of Lou Gehrig's disease, talking about the origin of the cosmos, the entire universe compacted within a singularity, a Black Hole. He found himself impressed, and momentarily skeptical. Yet he had no reason to doubt her; as far as he knew, she had always been forthright with him.

"I've come to think of it as a compensation, of sorts, for what happened to me." She touched a hand to her curled hair; despite the timing, he sensed no vanity in her gesture.

Off in the distance he could see tourists lined up to board one of the canal boats. Sunlight had broken through the overcast, providing the three remaining pigeons on the sidewalk with strutting shadows. One of the birds eyed him, seeking a handout.

At one low point in his career, with personal finances unraveling, he had been tempted to write a book about Joanne's experiences, but he'd never felt comfortable in his conscience with the exploitative aspect of it. And, too, there was his promise to Joanne's mother never to reveal the truth. Meeting Joanne again had briefly revived the idea; but from her manner he suspected she also would refuse permission. And despite her apparent lack of warmth, he liked the adult Joanne, just as he had felt a protective admiration for her as a child.

"Have you ever experienced any other, related incidents?"

"No. No more spinning mandalas, if that's what you mean. Nothing supernatural."

"I tried hard to locate you, you know," he said. "When your family moved the summer afterwards . . . Christ, the house wasn't even up for sale. By the time I managed to ferret out your new address, you'd move again, and I never could track you down. I tried just about everything short of hiring a private detective. Was that your mother's idea, to disappear like that?"

When she nodded he said, "I thought so."

He felt that there were a hundred other questions he wanted to ask now that he had finally found her, but for some reason he could not pinpoint even one. Finally, he asked the one question he thought might be most important to Joanne herself: "What happened that day . . . does it haunt you still, at all? Or has it faded into your past—lost some of its importance along the way?"

She laughed. And there was bitterness within her laughter, he thought. "Oh, it's still very much with me, all right. Vividly with me, every day of my life."

Unsure how to respond, he groped for the menu. "Would you like to join me for lunch? There's so much more I want to talk about. It's a shame we lost touch with—"

"No," she said, cutting him off. "No. I'm supposed to catch up with my sister . . . she's in one of the shops near here. It was nice seeing you again, though."

For the first time, as she stood, she turned fully toward him, meeting his gaze. He sensed defiance in the gesture, this sudden revealing of the asymmetry of her features, which she had formerly concealed from him. The right side of her face, *her* right side, was that of an adult. The other side was frozen in time, the face of the girl he had interviewed twelve years before, little changed. Both halves were comely, yet the mis-matched joining of the two crippled her beauty. Only the nose was perfect, with identical nares curving left and right, causing him to suspect the work of a cosmetic surgeon. He wondered whether further operations were planned.

"Good-bye, Dr. Bastian," she said. "Perhaps we'll see each other again." Her tone suggested the possibility unlikely.

"Good-bye, Joanne. Take care."

He hoped that she saw no pity or revulsion in his gaze. Of course she had seen the surprise. The shock. By no means was she hideous; but she was not the whole and beautiful woman she might have been.

She turned then walked away, limping. The left leg shorter than the right, and much thinner. The shorter leg stilted upward by a built-up shoe—like seeing a victim of polio in an era when the disease had all but vanished.

And as he watched the unbalanced gait of her departure, he attempted to recall, but could not, because his mind and his memory kept doing mirror reversals, whether it had been her right side or her left that had journeyed halfway through the wall; halfway into the mandala.

THE GUIDE
Richard Lee Byers

I SLIPPED OVER THE GRAVEYARD WALL A LITTLE AFTER DUSK, then spent a chilly three hours creeping through the shadows of the oaks and monuments. At last, when I'd begun to fear I'd missed my quarry, I spied him huddled on the ground at the feet of a marble angel. His vague form glimmered like fog in the moonlight.

Even after twenty years of playing this game, my mouth went dry, and my pulse ticked faster. Reminding myself that, dead or no, he was only a Gajo, I stepped into the open, touched the wide, black brim of my hat, and said, "Good evening, *Ray Baro*." He hadn't really been a "great lord" but the son of a mill owner, but the flattery helped put the proper oil in my tone.

His head snapped toward me. The blurry features sharpened, revealing a long nose, a small chin, and a startled expression; the hint of a cravat and lapels formed on his breast. He leaped up and turned to flee.

"Don't go!" I said quickly. "I'm a friend."

He pivoted back around. His face was still wary. "Who are you?" he asked. His voice was thin, like a failing echo.

"Just Yishwan," I said. "A humble Rom. For the last two days, my *kumpania* has been camped yonder." I gestured with my silver-inlaid cane. Naturally, I pointed in the wrong direction. "And you sir? Can you tell me who you are?"

His murky eyes blinked. "I . . . I think my name is David."

It was all I could do not to grin. Like many of the newly dead, he was addled, a circumstance that greatly improved my chances. "What are you doing in this lonely place?" I asked.

David spread his misty arms. "I don't know! At first, when I woke up, I was lying in some kind of box. I felt like I was being suffocated. I pushed at the lid, and suddenly I was here, wherever here is. I don't understand what's happening to me!"

"It's all right" I said. "I'll help you. We'll puzzle it out together."

"For a while, there was a circle of light, like the mouth of a tunnel opening in midair," David continued distractedly. "I had an urge to go in, but I was afraid. It seemed uncanny. But maybe I should have gone. I wonder if I could still find it."

"You mustn't try," I said. "We gypsies know about such things. They're like the will-o'-the-wisps that lead men to destruction in the marshes. There's nothing beyond the tunnel *except* light. No whist tables or pretty women. No crackling fires or elegantly cut suits to warm you, no soft armchairs or featherbeds to ease your bones. No juicy roasts to fill the hollow in your belly, or claret to wash the dryness from your throat." A fair enough picture of the next world, though misleading. But as my father always said, *tshatshimo Romano: the truth is expressed in Romani.* A man is free to claim what he likes in other tongues. "May the good God save you from such an inhospitable place."

Still looking dazed, David shook his head. "'It sounds horrible." By all accounts, he'd relished his pleasures. "But it's cold and horrible here, too."

"Of course it is," I said, "on a bleak and windswept hill. But no doubt you have a wealth of comforts awaiting you at home."

"Home," he murmured. A smile quirked his lips. "I think I recall a brick house with white shutters, rosebushes in front and a gazebo and stable in back." His mouth twisted. "But I don't know where it is!"

"Don't worry," I said. "I'll wager that, together, we can find it. Come on." I turned and strode away. David took a last, uncertain look around, then hurried after me. Muddleheaded and distraught as he was, he would have followed the Devil himself sooner than be left alone.

Wishing I were still as spry as when I was a *shav*—a youth—I clambered back over the fieldstone wall. David stepped through it without seeming to notice what he was doing.

Below us lay the town. At this late hour, most of the buildings were dark. Good. It wouldn't do to be seen in the company of a spirit.

We set off down the rutted dirt road. For a moment, David vanished, and I feared I'd lost him, but then he flickered back into view. Desiring to better assess his state of mind, I asked, "Do you remember *anything* of how you came to be up here?"

"No," he said glumly. "Wait, now I do! There was a sort of parade, and everything was black. The clothing, the horses, and the plumes on their heads. One sniffling old woman had dark crepe wrapped around her ear-trumpet. And it seemed like I was inside my box in one of the coaches, but marching alongside it at the same time." He faltered. "Except, how could that be?"

"I can't say, but I believe you." We entered the town, a motley sort of place where quaint old structures were giving way to the shabby tenements thrown up for the mill hands. I resolved to keep my voice down and my eyes peeled, lest we blunder into some *shanglo* on patrol. "Go on."

"The parade started at a church. Though I didn't understand what it was all about, I tried to memorize our route. Somehow I knew I wanted to be able to find my way back. But they kept turning corners, going in circles and doubling back, until I lost my bearings. Why would they do that?"

I shrugged, though of course I knew. All over the world, wittingly or not, people take such precautions, the most common being to blind a corpse with a shroud or a coffin and a covering of earth. Lest this prove insufficient, in the north of England the cortege goes roundabout. In Bohemia, the mourners wear masks. Other places, certain bodies are buried at crossroads. It's all magic meant to disorient the dead, to ensure that they won't follow their kin back home from the grave site.

But now and again, they do anyway, and sometimes it's thanks to a helpful fellow like me, who's made it his business to guide them.

We turned a corner. The shacks and cottages we'd been passing gave way to grander houses. And in the middle of the street lay the carcass of a black and white cat, its midsection crushed by a cart wheel. David gaped at it.

"Come along," I said.

"Dead," he whimpered. "I remember now. I'm dead."

In my thoughts, I cursed. I'd hoped to see him safely installed in his family home without ever having to deal with the unpleasant fact of his condition. God alone knew why the sight of a dead animal had roused his comprehension when the spectacle of his own funeral procession hadn't, but there it was. "Now stay calm," I said.

"*Dead!*" he wailed, then rounded on me. "What trick are you playing? What are you doing to me?"

I didn't think he'd attack me, or that his vaporous hands could harm me if he did. He wouldn't have discovered the trick of it yet. Still, it took an effort not to quail before the fury in his gaze. "Taking you home, just as I promised," I said. "Doing you a kindness, in the hope it will bring me luck. May you burn candles for me if it isn't so."

"But I don't belong at home. Not anymore."

"How would you prefer to spend eternity?" I asked. "Rotting in a lightless hole? Prowling a freezing lych-yard, with only nightjars and the moaning of the wind for company? Or warming yourself at your own familiar hearth, leeching a bit of carnal joy from the hearts of living men?"

"There was the tunnel—"

"It had already closed when I met you, remember, and perhaps that's just as well. Were you such a perfect Christian that you can be sure it wasn't the glare of hellfire shining through from the other side?"

"I don't know!" he said. "But I don't want to be here. I don't want anyone to see me. I don't want to think!" His gauzy form faded.

"Stop!" I said. "Don't you even want revenge?"

"What?" His substance thickened. "Do you mean that someone killed me?"

"Well, of course I don't *know*. Only you can say for certain, if you can ever dredge the truth out of your memory. But you weren't sick. There are rumors flying around the town."

David frowned. "I think there was a man who looks like me. Francis! My brother! The horses were tired, but he insisted on one more race. Star— my mount—couldn't make the jump. He fell on top of me, and I felt things break inside my chest."

"And now Francis's patrimony is twice as big as before."

"I know we had our quarrels, though I don't recall what they were about. But I'm sure he loved me! What happened must have been an accident!"

"If you say so," I said. "Then, as there's nothing to keep you, melt away into the dark if you feel you must. But first, wouldn't you like one last look at your home? It's only a few paces away. You'd already have recognized the neighborhood, if your dear brother hadn't taken pains to befuddle you."

David opened his mouth. I fancied he wanted to say no, but couldn't bring himself to speak the word.

"It's now or never," I warned. "You'll never find your way back by yourself."

"All right," David said. "Just for a second."

I led him up one lane and down another—in truth, it was a bit farther than I'd let on. At last the house rose up before us. A light shone in one of the ground-floor windows.

David stood and stared at the place, abject yearning in his face.

"Go closer," I said. "Look inside." Once again, I sensed he was struggling to refuse, but instead he slunk through the wrought-iron gate and up the cobbled drive. I hurried after him, keeping to the grass so no one in the house would hear me coming.

When I joined David at the window, I nearly crowed with glee. The tableau behind it could scarcely have been better if I'd staged it myself.

We were peeping into a luxurious parlor. Someone had stopped the ormolu clock on the mantel and turned the mirror to the wall, other practices meant to speed a departing spirit on its way. In a wing chair sat a smirking youth with a long nose like David's. He had a half-smoked cigar and a snifter of brandy on the table beside him, a giggling girl, probably one of the servants, on his lap, and a black armband slipping down his sleeve.

David glared at him. His clutching fingers gouged pocks in the windowsill. It was plain that he'd fallen prey to the envy and resentment the dead notoriously harbor against the living.

Myself, I didn't blame Francis for taking a bit of pleasure at the end of a doleful day. But what I whispered was: "Not very proper behavior, considering that you've only been in the ground a few hours. But perhaps this is in way of a victory celebration."

"He's has it all now," David said. "Everything that was mine."

"Then take it back," said I. "And while you're at it, punish him, and everyone else who betrayed you."

"I don't know how!"

"I promise, you'll find ways if you truly want to."

Points of foxfire glowed in the depths of his eyes. "I do."

Abruptly, he was gone. The wind howled, gusted, and shattered the window. The girl squealed, and Francis swore. I scurried into the shadows before they could get up and look outside.

Heading back to camp, I felt smug. The haunting had begun even better that I'd hoped. Of course, I didn't know precisely what would happen next. Perhaps Francis, beset by nightmares and apparitions, would consult a gypsy wise woman. Or maybe David would kill his family, or at least drive them out of the house, leaving the place empty and ripe for plundering. Whatever befell, there was gold in the offing. We Rom simply had to keep watch, and embrace our opportunities. As I cleared the edge of town, I started to whistle.

RAT FAMILIAR
Patricia Russo

THE BURNT CHILD CREPT INTO THE STORAGE SHED just before dawn. Mikis lay still as a stone, so deeply asleep not even the crash of crockery as she overturned a table nor the acrid stinks of the potions escaping from the broken jars woke him. He slept blackly, no glimmer of dream stirring his consciousness. It wasn't his fault. The witch had kept him awake for days, stoking and tending a curse-fire, and had released him from his labor only an hour ago.

The witch discovered the intruder shortly after sunrise; crouching in a corner, one bare, filthy foot bleeding from stepping on a shard. She stared wide-eyed from behind matted, soot-streaked hair as the witch snatched up a rusty poker and laid into Mikis. The child winced at each thud, but made no sound.

The fourth blow roused him. Seven times seven times seven years, he thought, before he even opened his eyes. His back, his shoulder, and his hip throbbed. His nose stung, and his eyes had watered in his sleep. A fifth blow slammed across his spine. The witch was beating him, he realized, and knew better than to roll away. "Yes," he gasped, then began to cough. "Yes. Yes. I serve." Seven times seven times seven years.

"You serve like a three-legged hound with his head in a sack," the witch shouted. She jabbed the poker toward the cringing child. "What's that?"

The girl let out a squeak.

Mikis took in the toppled table, the smashed jars. My work, he thought glumly. My sweat. The miserable creature in the corner ducked her head behind her arms.

"It's a child," he said. "I think."

"Get rid of it." The witch flung the poker at him. Mikis was already scrambling to his feet, and the length of metal struck him on the thigh. "Useless wretch," she spat.

"No no no!" the child shrieked, startling the both of them. Mikis felt a faint surprise that the witch could be startled. But her eyes widened and her lips thinned, and her body went very still.

Stupid brat. Foul, stupid child. When he took a step toward her, the girl jumped up. Thinking she was about to flee, Mikis halted. He didn't want to get in the way of that. Go on, go, idiot child, he urged silently.

The girl ran straight to the witch, holding out her arms like a toddler pleading to be picked up. A shiver of horror ran through him, and he cast his eyes around for the poker. Better for him to bash her head in quickly than anything the witch would do to her.

"Help me," the girl said. She stopped a few feet from the witch, holding her arms outstretched. Now Mikis saw the burns. Her inner arms were charred from wrist to elbow. Where the flesh hadn't been crisped black, it was red and raw and seeping. With a second shock, he saw that the insides of her spindly legs had also been burned. Her shift hid some of it, but it looked like both legs had been blistered from knee to thigh.

For a second he wondered what kind of accident could have befallen the child for her arms and legs to have been so badly and yet so evenly burned.

No. No accident. Whatever had happened to her had been done deliberately.

"Help me," she said again. Her voice was childishly thin, childishly high, but now that she was standing Mikis saw she wasn't as young as he'd first thought. Not eight or nine, but twelve or thirteen. Round-faced and blue-eyed, like any of a hundred peasant children in the valley. None of them had ever so much as set foot on the witch's property before, not in all the time Mikis had been with her. Their parents did, but only secretly and under the cover of night.

"Heal me," the girl demanded.

The witch's lips twitched. "Why?"

"Because you can."

The witch strode over to the girl and grasped her shoulders. Though the witch's nails dug into her flesh, she didn't flinch. The witch began to laugh. Not with malice or with scorn, but in delight.

◆　　◆　　◆

Vile child.

Silent, scowling, Mikis watched the girl scurry around the workroom. The witch murmured a soft word, and what she required was immediately in her hand. The girl smiled at him as she passed. Mikis's scowl deepened. She was always smiling. Always eager. She followed the witch around like a fawning pet.

Her arms had healed well. All that remained of her burns were a few faint, shiny scars. She was strong. She was helpful. Since her arrival, Mikis's workload had decreased greatly, and the witch paid almost no notice to him. That was good, because her notice invariably resulted in pain.

The girl didn't know that yet. Ela. She'd given her name to the witch as if it had no more worth than a scrap of paper, and seemed untroubled that the witch had never told her own. The witch, all mildness and warmth, gave her a bed in the house, offered her food four or five times a day, washed her, clothed her, and smiled upon her like a kindly grandmother. She had even plaited the girl's hair.

And now she was teaching her.

"Two parts lizardwort to three parts fever-root, steeped for nine days in the urine of a virgin boy . . . "

Ela murmured the witch's words under her breath, committing them to memory.

Mikis rubbed his jaw and frowned. Lies, all of it. Teaching her which plants must be gathered under the sun, which under the moon, which in full dark; drilling her patiently on the names of herbs and their uses; and now, pretending to instruct her in the preparation of simple potions. It was a lure, a sweet bait for the snare. She told the girl nothing of real use. No true cure or curse depended on herbs or decoctions, unguents or roots. The power was locked in the music of the spells, their sounds and rhythms, and the witch let not a syllable of even the most innocuous cantrip slip in Ela's hearing.

The witch had trapped him much less gently.

He'd been caught the instant he'd stepped into that glade. Much later, he realized the witch's real aim had been to ensnare him or someone like him, young, strong, healthy. She'd needed a new servant. She hadn't been hunting rabbits that day, but people.

Those happy rabbits, bounding to her where she sat in the grass, ignoring the stench of blood and entrails that hung over the glade, ignoring the skins pegged out to dry, unmindful of the pile of naked bodies beside her, had leapt into her lap as if eager to have their necks broken by her hand. Their eyes gleamed with contentment. As she gutted the last one, another hopped up to nestle on her lap. Blood sprayed over the newcomer's flanks as she tore the guts out of its predecessor, which must not have been quite dead. The rabbit on her laps twitched its ears, licked itself briefly, then settled back down happily, as unconcerned as if in its own burrow.

Stunned, awed, Mikis sank to his knees, his head swimming with the abattoir stink and the scent of sun-soaked grass and wild violets. And something else, too, which he only realized much, much later. "What?" he blurted.

She glanced at him coolly, her black eyes dead smudges in a doughy face. "Stew meat."

Already the chains had looped around him, already the snare had sprung. He felt no fear, only fascination. "No, no, my lady." (Remembering he had called her that, his face burned.) "I mean, how?"

"Safe," she said, dropping the limp, emptied carcass to tap out a soft rhythm on the ground. "Safe safe safe. That's what they hear."

Now Mikis sensed the rhythm himself, vibrating in the air, faint and soundless as the echo of a drum felt through a mile of earth. It reverberated in his bones. For a second, his eyes dazzled; he thought he saw a pattern of sparkles in the air, pulsing in time to the silent beat that shook him. He blinked, and it was gone.

"Safe," the witch said, grinning. She lifted the rabbit from her lap and broke its neck.

Mikis retained enough self-awareness to struggle when he felt the mesh of sparkles, more evanescent than the flashes he saw when he rubbed his closed eyes hard, but real, very real and icy cold, settle over him. He did not acquiesce like the rabbits, trusting and content. He fought, but the battle was over and lost in an instant.

"Seven times seven times seven," the witch murmured.

"What?" he groaned. His muscles were as slack as cut ropes. He lay on his side, drool trickling down his chin.

"Years. You will be mine for seven times seven times seven years."

He blinked. He could still blink. He could still move his lips. "Nobody lives that long."

The witch had let out a malicious chuckle.

Mikis watched Ela bustle around the workroom, and rubbed his face again. The witch's slyness with the girl disturbed him. No spell enmeshed her, no invisible chains bound Ela to the witch's will. Yet. Mikis wondered what she was waiting for.

Ela smiled again as she passed him, the smile faltering as she took in his expression. The witch's back was turned, her head bent as she stirred something noxious over a small fire in the hearth. That had always been his job.

Mikis raised his hand, and the girl stopped. She wanted to move away, wanted to hurry back to the witch's side, he knew. Mikis fixed his gaze on hers, then flicked his eyes toward the door. *Go*, he mouthed. He shaped the words with exaggerated care, so there could be no mistake. *Get out. Run.*

He knew she understood. Her face went pale. She glanced at the door, fleetingly, fearfully. *Witch*, he mouthed, with a tiny gesture toward the hearth. But surely the girl knew that. It was the reason she'd come here in the first place.

Ela made a face at him. It was almost a sneer.

"Ela? Is anything wrong?" The witch suddenly loomed over the girl's shoulder. Mikis, petrified, clenched his teeth and stared at his hands so as not to meet her eyes.

"No, nothing," the girl said, sweetly.

"Is my homunculus disturbing you? Is my rat familiar making a nuisance of itself?" The witch slapped Mikis hard.

"Rat familiar?" Ela repeated, wonderingly.

"You didn't think he was a person, did you?" She struck Mikis again, with her fist this time. "Look at that face. Look at those limbs. It's just a big, stretched-out rat."

"I'm not," Mikis mumbled. He tasted blood.

"I just keep it around for amusement."

Liar, he wanted to scream. You bound me to you to do your work. To haul and sweat for you, to serve and serve and serve. Seven times seven times seven . . .

Mikis reared up. The witch hit him, and he staggered, but fixed his eyes on Ela. She looked back, horrified. "Slave," he said, dribbling blood. "I'm her slave." And so will you be if you stay here much longer. He hoped she could see the warning in his face, for he dared not say it aloud.

Ela's horror-struck expression deepened. Mikis thought he had made her understand, until he realized it wasn't the witch she was horrified of, but him.

*　　·　　·

Mikis woke in the darkness of the storage shed, in the grip of a nausea so severe he began to retch before he could turn over on his side. It made no difference; there was nothing in his stomach to come up. The witch hadn't fed him for three days; the hungrier he got, the sicker he felt.

The witch's doing, of course. She'd long ago spelled that weird on him, to prevent him stealing food. As long as he ate regularly he was fine, but even one missed meal roused a gripping, griping nausea. Many times, he thought she delayed feeding him on purpose, because she enjoyed watching him try to force food down when his stomach was in a roil.

Groaning softly, he got to his knees. This time, he knew she'd simply forgotten, all her attention taken up with the girl. Mikis hadn't dared to ask for anything to eat. He'd rather suffer days of the dry heaves than invite another beating.

Or so he'd thought. He couldn't stand it any more. Though the idea of food made him retch so violently he couldn't catch his breath, he knew it was the only cure. But if he woke the witch to beg her to open the larder, she'd kill him. And if she caught him helping himself, or noticed so much as a crumb missing, she'd . . .

If only killing him were the worst she could do.

Kill him, blast him, flay him and put his skin back inside out, turn him truly into a rat—Mikis decided anything would be more endurable than another minute of this wrenching, roiling nausea. Hunched over and shivering, he crept out of the shed and made his way to the house, so lost in his own misery he didn't hear the witch and Ela talking until he was almost upon them.

They were in the workroom. Mikis crouched, panting, terror for a moment driving all bodily ills from his mind. They weren't talking.

They were working a spell.

Together.

Ela's voice, though tentative, wove the counterpoint around the witch's melody. Mikis recognized the spell from its shape; they were creating a simple ward, a bubble of power to repel minor threats.

"Very good," the witch said warmly. "Now you try it alone."

Ela began, then stopped abruptly. "Wait. Someone's outside."

Mikis, terrified, scuttled to the shed and secreted himself in the straw. The witch entered a few minutes later, Ela on her heels, and beat him for not alerting her to an intruder. "I'm sick," he cried, as she laid into him with the poker. "I'm hungry."

"He's not a very good watch dog," Ela observed. "Or watch rat."

The witch laughed. The sound of it caused Mikis more pain than the blows landing across his shoulders. "True, but not to worry. I've been thinking about getting a new one anyway. We'll pick one out together, shall we?"

Mikis gurgled a protest.

"What is it, rat?" Ela asked.

Mikis retched, and retched again. "Seven times seven times . . . "

"Yes," the witch murmured, turning him over with her foot. "It'll be interesting to see what's left of you after all that time."

♦   ♦   ♦

Over the next couple of weeks, the witch deigned to feed him almost as much as he needed, but otherwise ignored him. Mikis spent most of his time in the shed, sick and afraid. Whenever he thought about what the witch had said, his heart galloped so rapidly he thought it would burst.

In his calmer moments, he knew she had lied. It hadn't been that long; he had not served out even a fraction of the term of years for which she had bound him. He would have noticed. He would have realized.

Nobody lived that long.

And if he were that old, then how old was she?

No. It was just another one of her lies, another one of her cruelties. He'd stepped into that glade only . . . not last summer, he knew it was longer ago than that. Five years ago? Maybe five. No more than ten. It could not be that the only thing keeping him from collapsing into a heap of dust was the spell woven around his body, that mesh he'd seen sparkle in the air the instant before it closed around him, and whose rhythm he still felt as a dull, intermittent twinge in his bones.

He tried to believe that.

Seven times seven times seven was . . .

No.

Footsteps. Mikis squeezed his eyes shut, pretending to be asleep. The door creaked open; he held himself very still. But the person moving around the shed was treading too lightly, too tentatively, to be the witch. Ela.

"She stole my life," he said.

The footsteps stopped. "I'm looking for the lamb's-fat candles."

"She stole my life and she'll steal yours, too."

"I need those candles." Away from the witch, Ela was much more subdued than in her presence. Biting her lip, she rubbed her hands together nervously.

"Get out of here while you can," he said. "At night, when she's asleep. Sneak away. And never come back."

"I can't," she whispered.

"Why not?" Her timidity made him bold; that he'd dared speak at all made his heart beat painfully. Bold and scared, he said, "You're not bound. I can tell. You've got to go before she does bind you."

"She won't. She told me. Where are those damn candles, rat?" But her voice shook, and the kick she aimed at him was feeble.

"Get out of here," he repeated.

"No. You're wrong. You're *stupid*. She's not going to make me like you. She's teaching me. I'm going to be like *her*."

"Is that any better?" he asked.

Ela flushed. She kicked him again, hard. Her eyes filled, and she wiped them quickly, brushing the tears away before they fell. Angrily, she yanked up her sleeves to show her scars. "Could be worse," she said. "I know what worse is. I'm not going back to that."

The small hope Mikis had nurtured drained from him. He stared at the floor. Tugging down her sleeves, Ela remained where she was standing, as if waiting for something. The candles, thought Mikis, she wants me to tell her where they are. But when he looked up, her eyes were full of tears, and this time she hadn't brushed them away.

"I know you're not a rat," she said. "I know that was a lie. I'll make her let you go. I promise."

Let me go? The words sang in his head. Let me go to what? She thought slavery preferable to freedom because of what awaited her outside the witch's domain. For Mikis, there was nothing outside the witch's domain, nothing but emptiness, oblivion, his long-postponed death.

It terrified him.

If only Ela would run away. Then the witch would have to keep him.

"The lamb's-fat candles are in that chest over there, behind the door," Mikis said. She bobbed her head and hurried over to the chest. It took her a moment to get the catch open and raise the lid. When she bent to reach the bundle of candles at the bottom of the chest, Mikis crushed the back of her skull with the poker.

The witch punished him with fire and punished him with cold; she blistered his blood and rotted his bones; she bubbled his marrow, rent his flesh, shredded every nerve. She punished him for seven times seven times seven days, and Mikis screamed for every minute of every hour of those three hundred and forty-three days. At the end of it she put him back together again, for more than a year of lifting and hauling and stirring and sweating for herself had worn down her rage.

But despite all her skill and power, she could not restore Mikis to his former state. The best she could manage was an elongated creature which resembled nothing so much as a stretched-out rat. It was useless for her purposes, and after the witch captured a pair of young hikers and bound them firmly and well, she let her weeping rat familiar collapse into dust.

EMPATHY
Jeffrey Thomas

THEY WOULD CALL IT A MURDER-SUICIDE, though it was never fully understood. Perhaps it was one, actually—in its way. Or perhaps it wasn't just that Marie empathized with the things at *Blue Flamingos*, but they with her.

Blue Flamingos Antiques and Collectibles was the name Edwin, Marie's husband, had given the three-story brick warehouse, and it was a blue-painted lawn flamingo he had placed in the front window beside the blue lava lamp, though he could as easily have called it Pink Elephants or Flying Aardvarks to get his point across.

There were certainly enough traditional antiques to draw serious collectors, and some of them were willing to part with serious money. The vast ground floor was nearly as neatly laid out as a department store, with tables and counters and shelves, corridors built of merchandise. Clean, well-preserved merchandise; this was no flea market. Edwin had had his name, and the name *Blue Flamingos*, printed in a magazine article several years ago in commemoration of the hundredth anniversary of the jukebox.

Empathy

It was tacked up by the cash register, his brief quote on the restoration of jukeboxes circled.

But it was the collectibles rather than the antiques for which the place was best known. The article could indicate that. Edwin was a collector of '50s paraphernalia. Art Deco furniture. Old radios; a whole tall shelf just of those in the darker, quieter, somewhat less orderly second story. Primitive futuristic TVs, the sad, unlit shells of arcade games, the colorless, translucent bones of neon signs. Items so odd and unique that people were willing to drive here from Boston sometimes for the chic junk of yesterday. Art Deco, old radios and jukeboxes were always hip, but also a few years ago there had been the resurgence of interest in the '60s, and *Blue Flamingos* had done well for that. College kids in abundance, no doubt feeling very hip when they punched up old Roy Orbison songs on the gorgeously gaudy replica Wurlitzer 1015 by the counter where you first came in, drawn to it moth-like, like kids in the '40s, mindlessly lured by the green, orange, yellow plastic colors, the water bubbles tumbling corpuscle-like through lurid veins. Lights, movement, noise; a carnival in a futuristic sarcophagus, now a sacred American icon . . . the predecessor of the TV, and MTV. Today's mall mentality served Edwin well. The allure of *things*.

And Marie's husband knew what they wanted because he loved these things as they did. He might not have been able to part with any of it, jealous collector that he was, if there wasn't a constant stream of new things coming in to replace those that left. Flea Markets, field auctions. He read obituaries, contacted relatives about the possessions of deceased parents and grandparents. College kids and Bostonians didn't know where to go, and didn't want the bother of that anyway. They would pay double, triple and more for their cherished junk, while throwing away the stuff they bought in the malls, the treasure of tomorrow's scavengers.

"It's like the ultimate attic!" one woman enthused to Edwin at the counter, paying thirty dollars for a Barbie doll he had acquired for five dollars, along with three others in a box of toys at a yard sale.

From across the room, dusting variegated displays that would make the Smithsonian's attic collections boring by contrast, Marie watched as

73

Edwin smiled at the woman and offered some obligatory banalities. Edwin wasn't very good with small talk, just with the large talk of his drinking companions. Basically, Marie's husband preferred things to the human beings that made them. But then, who didn't?

◆   ◆   ◆

As every day, after showering and cleansing herself, Marie set about polishing and cleaning the other, inanimate tenants of *Blue Flamingos*.

Marie had just finished dusting a baby alligator, which reared on its hind legs like some mummified miniature dinosaur, now extinct. The bright pink feathers of the duster had snared on its grin of fangs and Marie dislodged them delicately with an apologetic smile. Lightly, with the ball of her thumb, she wiped the dust off its unblinking black eyes.

Marie also cherished the many things collected in her husband's shop. She often felt more pained than he to see them leave. But hers was not the love of a collector. Marie had never collected anything in her life. As a deaf child, living in a school for deaf children during the week and with her mother in a two room apartment on weekends, she hadn't had the room—the private space—to accommodate the luxury of collection. Marie was fond of malls in the way she was fond of museums. She loved to drink it all in, then went home full. She was not materialistic. She loved the collectibles and old things because they were bits and pieces of *lives*. She could see and smell the life—the love, often—still in them, soaked deeply in their pores from the hands of their owners. Now discarded, orphaned by unsentimental survivors of those gone before. They were sad things. Lonely things. Of course, she should feel happy to see them all here together in her home. She felt as one with them. She felt empathy with these dustily alive things.

Edwin had disgustedly given in to her pleading, for a while, to let her keep a certain old doll or teddy bear or children's book, to bring it up to their apartment on the third floor, which for its decor could very easily have been mistaken for part of the store. But now he told her she had enough things, and he had a business to run. He made her feel guilty for her sensitivity, made her wonder if she really had gone overboard with it. He mocked her, for instance, for no longer accompanying him to field auctions because she couldn't bear to see the boxes of rain-soggy stuffed animals, once warm with children's hugs, and the rest of the things left for junk in the field after the bidders had picked what they really wanted from the boxes they bought—a corpse-strewn, muddy battlefield.

What Marie didn't tell her husband, however, was that she mostly didn't accompany him because she sensed that he didn't really desire her company. He no longer offered to buy her a hot dog under the snack pavilion. No longer talked to her on the way home.

You would think that he didn't know how to communicate with a deaf woman. He had attended classes for signing when they first met five years ago, knew how to sign perfectly well . . . but that would require him to show too much of an interest in her. His brusque signs now were more like impatient gestures of dismissal than sign language.

It was a rainy October day today, and in fact Edwin was at an auction, so perfectly scheduled for such weather. Marie wandered now throughout the second floor, dusting. The shop was tended presently by Mrs. Morris, who couldn't sign a jot and thus moved her mouth with ludicrous exaggeration so Marie could read her lips.

Dangling from the high ceiling were antlers and pop guns, catcher's mitts and musical instruments. Marie worked her way toward the back, dusting the rows of uglier, less artistic steel and glass jukeboxes of the '50s and '60s. She had once been afraid to come up here alone, before she had dared to let herself feel this was her home. Now when she occasionally glanced over her shoulder, it was only because she felt Edwin would be standing there, arms crossed, some complaint ready. The sad deer head, the fluorescent, crumbling paper-mâché ghoul from a carnival horror ride didn't mean her any harm.

At the end window she gazed down at the rain-blurred street. A young couple were running toward the building, his coat spread over both their heads. They were laughing. Marie smiled. Marie herself was only twenty-five. Edwin was a decade older. She wondered if that was part of his change. Maybe he resented her youth. Maybe subconsciously the discard he saw on days like today ate at him too . . . reminded him of his mortality, and the fact that he would never be remembered as a Barbie doll or Wurlitzer 1015 is remembered.

As she did every day, now that she accepted the fact that her husband no longer loved her, Marie tried to fathom his change. The rain helped her abstract and liberate her thoughts, and to travel back in time.

He had never been a sunny man. She had made the error, as so many women do, of mistaking surliness for sexiness. And his artistic air had been even easier to interpret as romantic. For Edwin's true desire had been to be a painter. He hadn't painted in two years. When she first knew him he would still contribute to the town's annual art show, and sold the occasional piece. But even before Marie had met him he had given up trying to get backing for his own show. Now he had retreated to his world of things, no longer attempting to create new things of his own. Maybe, Marie wondered, he even resented his collections for the preservation and interest he and his art would never know in future times. Or maybe vicariously he sought longevity through association. But it was all connected. Art was things too, and it was with mute things that Edwin best interacted. Because he didn't seek true interaction. He just wanted to paint himself into an environment worthy of his complex identity. He had boasted to one drinking buddy that he was a cross between Salman Rushdie and Cat Stevens. He was *misunderstood*, and played that angry song by the Animals on the bogus Wurlitzer frequently. The booming vibration would rumble in Marie's chest.

Marie hurriedly finished up so she could return downstairs and steal peeks at the attractive young couple. They didn't notice her at first, so stealthy was she in her own silence, but the girl gave her a glance. The boy gave her a glance and a second glance with a smile tossed in. Marie was beautiful—dark haired, full-lipped, the lips ever sealed into a unit, it seemed, though she could speak in her difficult way when she occasionally chose. Large-breasted, small and slender. God, in His wise-guy's wisdom, had given her all but the ability to hear. She would have deflated her breasts for that. But then, would Edwin have married her, had she been less attractive, though hearing? She doubted it, these days. Doubted it severely. Simply because his passion for her body was as strong now as it had been five years ago. He held onto her in his private collection for that reason alone.

Maybe he had collected her for that reason alone in the first place, though now he was better able to cut his motivation down to its reality, uncluttered by pretenses to love and affection. Yes—maybe he had never loved her. Watching the couple leave the store, Marie had tears in her eyes. No, he loved me, part of her countered desperately, almost panicking at the thought. But he's grown more and more bitter with life. He's close to me, and that's why he can take it out on me.

Did she believe that? She certainly wanted to. But in recent months, she had come to feel that she had always been just another blue flamingo in Edwin's collection. A glorified, extra realistic blow-up doll you didn't need to talk to, who couldn't voice complaint. A beautiful mannequin, to be put away with the rest of the attic treasures when not in use.

Deaf friends Marie had known in school, but now lost track of, had been feisty, taught to be independent and bold. But in others, the world crushed that, like a tank over a foot soldier. Friday, for instance, Marie had driven to the market to do the weekly grocery shopping. On the way to and from, impatient drivers cut her off, rode her tail, swore at her and thumped their wheels in frustration at her careful driving. In the store, she had to ask the man at the deli counter a question three times in order to read his lips, and she had read at last, "What are you, stupid?" A woman banged Marie's hip with her cart without apology. Another, whose cart blocked the way, wouldn't move it when Marie asked, forcing her to move the woman's cart herself, in a rare act of strength. Another woman had glared and actually pulled her child away when Marie patted its head. It was all just little things. But so many, and every day. This was common life. They could do this, though they would hate to have it done to them. They simply did not empathize with one another, so obsessed were they with their own destinations and needs and desires.

Handicaps didn't bring out the best in people, either, she had found . . . but the worst. They activated the pecking order syndrome. The abolition of the weak, the mutant. They couldn't empathize with that, because they didn't want to imagine themselves that way. Acknowledge their frailty and mortality. So it was now, also, with the handicap of age. Old things were hip, but old people weren't. The mutely strutting models on MTV were desirable objects, but not the silent reality. Edwin had once told Marie, when drunk and lofty-mouthed, that Renoir nudes didn't sweat, didn't have periods. Marie remembered that now and cemented her conviction once and for all.

Which hurt, because, either out of programmed masochism or simply the need to feel important to at least one person in this world, Marie still loved him.

◆   ◆   ◆

It had taken Marie a while to figure out why she had such empathy for the stuffed alligator. Her feelings for the toys and knick-knacks made more sense. Maybe because it had once been truly alive. And a baby, too. But there was a stuffed iguana, gray, its mouth filled with red-painted plaster, and some trophy heads of higher animals. It had to be that the thing was so shocking to see, its condition so cruelly unnatural and humiliating. The alligator was positioned so as to stand on its hind legs and tail, a foot tall that way. In its outstretched arms, like Oliver Twist, it proffered a wooden bowl, presumably as a change holder. Maybe candy, depending on its artist's perversity. Its hands were fastened to the bowl with nails; reptilian stigmata, a Lizard King of Kings. In its mouth it clamped a red light bulb. It was a table lamp. It was the bizarre and grotesque lengths someone had gone to that so disgusted Marie, and made her hurt for the thing. Like a shrunken head, or a lamp shade made from a Jew. A blasphemous work of art.

Staring at it, she turned the bulb on. Red light painted her face, and made red pupils in the creature's ebon eyes. She fantasized about burying the tortured creature. Looking up, she was startled to see Edwin there smiling at her derisively. He was late back from the auction, and he'd been drinking already. "I'll cry the day I have to part with that beauty," he told her, though not in sign language. "I should just take it upstairs."

"It's horrible and sick," Marie signed to him. She hadn't wanted to use the intimate awkwardness of her voice with him for weeks now.

"I saw you mooning over it. Don't get disgusted at me; I didn't kill the thing." Edwin joined Mrs. Morris behind the counter. "I've loved that thing since I saw it," he told the older woman. "Freaky."

"You like the freaky, Ed," she replied distractedly, otherwise occupied. Though she didn't exaggerate her mouth's movements, Marie could read her lips.

"When I was young you could still go to a carnival and see those deformed babies in bottles they called pickled punks, before somebody made a stink about transporting dead bodies over state lines. If I could find any of them today I'd buy them and put them upstairs for sure. How's that for freaky?"

"Yuck."

"Marie." He looked up at her. "I'm wet; go make me a cup of coffee, will ya?" He was good-naturedly ugly from drinking and from coming back empty-handed from the hunt.

Marie didn't doubt at this moment that Edwin would also buy a shrunken head or a lamp shade of human skin if he could find them. She shut off the bulb and moved to the stairs.

Freaky, her mind echoed.

.   .   .

The smell of sex always seemed to repulse Edwin afterwards, so he went to take one of his long, languid baths with a paperback and a Scotch Marie brought to him. She left him and went down into the store, to sit by the shelf of old books and read in her own manner . . . maybe to fill the void of emptiness inside her with something at least dustily alive.

She chose a book she had browsed through repeatedly recently, a volume of poetry by Thomas Hardy. There was a poem there she had read last time, and she looked for it again. As she flipped through, she glanced up at the alligator standing on the glass counter beside her. She felt the strange desire to change the red bulb to a normal one, and have the creature light her reading for her. An intimacy rather than an exploitation. She didn't do it. She had found the poem: *The Mongrel.*

The rain droned on outside as Marie read. Mrs. Morris had long since gone home, to discover the bodies tomorrow upon her return.

The poem told the story of a man who could no longer afford to keep his dog, and so threw a stick into the water to trick it into drowning itself. The dog's naive trust and love showed in its eyes as it bravely tried to paddle back to shore, the stick in its mouth. Finally it succumbed, however, sucked under by a strong current . . . but in dying, and realizing the treachery of its master in the face of its own unswerving loyalty, a look of contempt for the whole human race came into its eyes. Like a curse, said Hardy.

Marie empathized with the dog.

She shut the book. The salt in her tears burned the vulnerable surfaces of her eyes. She was moments from being swept under. Now she allowed herself to feel the hatred she had been repressing. It felt like a curse.

Marie rested a hand on her thigh. In Maine as a child, when she was still considered retarded rather than deaf, a baby-sitter had purposely ground her heel into the top of that hand while Marie was playing on the floor . . .

And the thigh under her hand—Edwin had once kissed it, run his tongue along it. Well, he still did. But he had also crushed that thigh in his hand recently while they were in the car, so upset had he become at her driving. He hadn't hit her—Yet. Marie felt that first blow moving toward her through time. The bruises from his grip had taken days to fade . . .

Marie rose from the chair, slid the book back into the shelf. At a table close by she stood and gazed down at the unique items spread there. A tarnished pocket watch. Costume jewelry. Several ivory-handled straight razors, the blades old and brittle but still frighteningly sharp . . .

She sat back down beside the glass counter where the alligator stood, an array of African tribal masks hanging above it like an audience of spirits. Marie didn't mind their company. They were a comfort, in fact. They could lead her away, if they wanted. She rolled up the sleeves of her bathrobe, hating the smell of sex on her now also, and anxious to escape it. She *wanted* to drown like the dog, in salt tears. In blood. She cursed the frail impermanence of humankind, which caused so much greedy fear. She would have plenty of time to let this happen; Edwin would remain in the tub for two hours or more, soaking himself outside and in. She reached out to the alligator . . . somewhat guiltily . . . and flicked on its light so as to wash out the vivid color when it came—but it was intimacy, not exploitation.

·　　·　　·

Mrs. Morris found Marie, and the horror of it made her scream. Pale as she was, Marie looked like a mannequin propped in her chair. Mrs. Morris screamed for Edwin, and bolted upstairs to wake him . . .

In the open doorway of the bathroom, Mrs. Morris screamed a second time.

It was a perverse way to kill a man, the police said when they came. As perverse in imagination as the creation of that lamp in the first place. First they found a wooden bowl in the threshold of the bathroom. Then in the tub they observed the male corpse. He had died by electrocution, the cord of the lamp plugged into an outlet close at hand. But rather than simply toss the alligator lamp in there with him, the woman had gone to the trouble of stabbing the nails which protruded from the creature's palms into the sides of her husband's neck, so that the creature seemed to be strangling him.

But the sequence of all this was confusing. There was no great splashing of blood in the bathroom, so she had to have slit her wrists after the electrocution. How, then, or when, had the woman managed that other bizarre flourish . . . that of wetting the hind feet of the alligator in her blood, and tracking its prints up two flights of stairs and on into the bathroom? "Freaky," the policemen said, in disgust of her.

—For Rose

THE VEHICLE
Brian Lumley

I.

POWER-CELLS WEAKENED IN AN ACCIDENTAL EMERGENCE from hyper-space too close to one of the void's ultimate omnivores, a Black Hole, then almost completely drained in a further desperate jump to avoid the Hole's awful attraction, the tiny Hlitni craft reluctantly flickered back into three-dimensional being a few moments and several thousand light years later within Sol's system of nine planets. Brakes straining to capacity, it whipped in past the third world's satellite, drilled through the planet's atmosphere without raising a single blister on its completely heat-resistant skin, finally slowed and hovered six feet above the muddy bank of an English stream in a densely wooded area.

It hovered for only a second or so, then the cells gave up their last spark of life and the spaceship fell with a plop into the mud. It landed a few inches short of the water and close to the bank's spiky tufts of grass, lying there static and half-submerged. Inside the cone-shaped ship the crew was at emergency stations, separated—by human standards of comparison—by distances of hundreds of yards. All of this within the six-inch spike that was the ship.

Their communication system—telepathy, boosted mechanically by a device totally independent of the main power-cells—was still working; the Hlitni conversed:

"*Sarl, Klee? Are you two functioning?*"

"*Yes, Inth,*" Sarl came back, "*I'm functioning.*"

"*Me, too,*" reported Klee.

"*Good,*" Inth said, then asked: "*Sarl, what's the damage?*"

"*None that I can scan. We came down fairly soft.*"

"*And Klee, how's power—or shouldn't I ask?*"

"*You shouldn't ask, Inth. We're drained . . .*"

There was a pause, then: "*That bad, eh?*"

"*That bad, yes,*" Klee answered, "*but perhaps not desperate. It depends.*"

"*There are many power sources on this world, yes!*" Sarl, the youngest member excitedly reported. "*Before we fell I scanned tremendous energy expenditure!*"

"*We all did,*" Inth said. "*But the nearest source was at some distance—and we no longer have a vehicle . . .*"

Immediately, fearfully, Sarl and Klee scanned the ship's vehicle where it hung suspended in its cocoon. As Inth had so bluntly pointed out, the vehicle was dead. The cocoon's life-support system had depended upon energy bled off direct from the power-cells. Within it a creature like a tiny butterfly—only half-an-inch long but still many times larger than all three crew members together—lay with its wings and body contorted, grotesque in rigor mortis.

Finally, after a pause to let the implications sink in, Inth continued: "*There you have the problem in a hyondle—and it certainly doesn't look any too good. But we're not finished yet. Look, let's get together and see what we can scan.*"

"*Where there's a force.*" Sarl added, trying to sound cheerful but not quite making it, "*there's a function.*"

The Vehicle

"I do believe, Sarl," said Klee dryly, *"that if your antennae started to fray and your carapace developed cracks, you'd still be optimistic!"* Nothing more was said until they convened some minutes later in the recreation room.

II.

When Harry "the Hit" Coggin saw the police roadblock up ahead, he attempted to do a graceful, unconcerned, controlled left turn off the road onto a farm track. Which would have been fine except the track gate was tied not quite fully open, and Harry's borrowed car was a fraction too wide.

The police had spotted him in any case, and as he threw open the door of the car—its nose now deep in a ditch, along with the shattered wooden frame and bars of the gate—three of them set off at a run in his direction. Harry had no gun, or he might well have stood his ground and attempted to shoot them down before they could tackle him. They were unarmed, but that wouldn't have bothered Harry Coggin. Instead he set off along the track as fast as he could go, heading for the woods which started just beyond the small farm at the track's end.

He was still wearing the drab grey garb of the prison, but that was no handicap; compared with the smart uniforms of the policemen, Harry's loose-fitting prison clothes gave him ample freedom of movement. Truth to tell, the men pursuing him were not too eager to catch up with him. They were putting just enough effort into it to satisfy their superiors back at the roadblock. And their hesitancy was hardly difficult to understand.

Harry "the Hit" Coggin stood seventy-seven inches tall and weighed two hundred and forty pounds, and not one wasted. For two years a rare combination of native intelligence and sheer brawn had made him un-disputed king of the underworld, and during that time he had earned his nickname many times over. Then his luck had run out: he was caught red-handed and jailed for life for a double-murder of extreme savagery. Since then, at a top-security prison, he had indulged almost fanatically in athletic exercise, and his constant displays of strength and physical agility in the exercise yard had kept warders and fellow prisoners alike gaping in awe.

No, his three immediate pursuers were hardly putting heart and soul into their task, but why should they? No doubt Harry would hole-up in the woods, and then the dogs would be brought in, and that would be that . . . Completely painless, for everyone except Harry.

By now the fugitive was past the farm and entering the woods. He paused to get his bearings, catch his breath, look back. It looked pretty good. Even if those three coppers caught up with him they could do nothing. He was in tip-top condition and full of grim determination; he didn't intend to be taken again, not easily at any rate.

He clenched his fists and gritted his teeth. It would almost be worth letting them catch up with him...but no, however enjoyable the prospect, that would be a waste of precious time. What he had to do was find a decent hideout until nightfall, which was only a few hours away, and then make his way to one of the three neighboring villages. It wouldn't be easy, and doubtless before very long there would be a cordon with dogs, but Harry Coggin was no fool. He had friends up north, friends who were expecting him. If he could only lay his hands on another car . . .

He plunged on into the woods, altering the course of his flight to take him more nearly north. The woods, he knew, were almost five miles through at this point. In less than an hour he should be through to the opposite side. The law would be there, too, and long before him, but he would see them first. Then it would be touch and go until the fall of dark. It would help if he could find a decent place to hole-up. With this thought in mind he came out of the trees onto the bank of a long, narrow pool. Reeds grew tall and lush at the water's edge; the place would be a haven for moorhens. It would also be a good spot to throw the dogs off the trail.

Without hesitating he waded out through the reeds and mud and struck out across the pool. The water was cool and it freshened him up a bit. On the far side he quickly squeezed his shirt and trousers dry before moving on. Way back at the edge of the woods, Harry knew that the enemy would be calling up reinforcements: police dogs, trackers. But right here and now he was alone. Completely alone in the heart of the woods, with only the cooing of wood-pigeons and leaf-dappling rays of penetrating sunlight to keep him company . . . so why the hell did he keep thinking someone was watching him?

III.

And in fact someone was watching Harry "the Hit" Coggin, three some-ones—or somethings. Inth, Sarl and Klee were scanning him closely, try-ing to make something of him. Quite obviously Harry was not a power source in himself—not one that the aliens could tap, anyway—but he could doubtless take one of them to a power source, and then he could be made to bring the source back to the ship.

For of course to them Harry was simply a vehicle, far vaster than any they had ever come across before in their galaxy-spanning voyagings, and far more intelligent. Handling him or any other of his kind would be a far different hash of khrumm to handling the simple vehicles they were used to, but they were equipped for it; it should not prove impossible.

In fact they admired Harry, for certainly he was a very powerful ve-hicle indeed. Oh, they had scanned other potential vehicles in the woods, hundreds, thousands of them, and all apparently controllable. But Harry was fast-moving, extremely strong, and unlikely—they thought—to fall prey to natural enemies.

Then, as they continued to scan him, he started to veer away from them at an angle that would take him past them at too great a distance. There was only one thing for it. Perhaps the three of them together could exercise a measure of external control. With one of their own vehicles there would be no problem, but with this one . . . ?

They would have to see . . .

Harry was most surprised to find his feet going contrary to his mind. He had made up the latter just a few minutes earlier to skirt a steep, heav-ily overgrown hill in front by diverting slightly north-west. Indeed, he had already begun to change his course to circumvent the obstacle. Yet now—why!—here he was scrambling up through gorse, saplings, bracken and tall ferns, leaning forward to maintain his balance as he negotiated the steep slope, having returned almost without knowing it to his original course. Now what the hell . . . ?

The fugitive paused for a moment—just a moment—and the creases in his forehead deepened. Then he shrugged, gritted his teeth and carried on climbing. It must be sheer, animal instinct, he told himself. And he trusted his instincts. Come to think of it, the hill was quite a high one; from the top he should have an excellent view of the woods to his rear.

A few minutes later Harry reached the top, but by then he had apparently forgotten all about his plan to use the high place as an observation point. He had almost forgotten about the policemen, too, who might be hot on his trail . . . but not quite. Obviously, (he told himself) it was the sure knowledge that they were back there somewhere that drove him on, ever faster, through the woods. And yet (strange, unaccustomed sensation) it seemed almost as if some mind other than his own now guided his powerful piston legs. Again Harry frowned, and again he gave a mental shrug. He was going in the right direction, wasn't he?

IV.

"*Klee*," Inth said in his most casual manner, which was a sure sign that something was bothering him, "*have you by any chance scanned the ship since we came down? Have you studied its buoyancy, perhaps?*"

Klee fractionally relaxed his part of the trio's telepathic control on the still distant fugitive and prepared to scan the ship. Inth stopped him short: "*No, don't waste the effort. Allow me to tell you that we are sinking. Slowly but very surely, we are going down into the mud, and unless we can appreciably increase our prospective vehicle's speed . . . then our chances of ever leaving this backwater world are slim indeed.*" He paused to let that last sink in, then added: "*Of course, the biped can be exerted to the full—expended in an all out effort—once we get Sarl astride his brain . . .*"

"*Then we'd better start scanning for the nearest compact power source,*" Klee nervously answered. "*And we'd better start hoping that our vehicle,*" *when we've got him, is strong enough to carry that power source back to us. It would be too bad for us if Sarl burnt him out before we got the job done!"*

Harry was down the hill now, and his stride lengthened as he bounded between trees and crashed through thickets. In the back of his mind somewhere a voice kept asking him if he was crazy, and dully, knowing that he was talking to himself, he kept answering that he must be! But he was still headed in the right direction, and he was certainly covering ground faster than any policeman could. So why was he worrying?

The answer was simple, and when it occurred to Harry he deliberately grabbed at the bole of a tree and halted his headlong flight. For a moment the fog lifted from his brain, allowing him to see things clearly. He was worrying because this wasn't the way he'd planned it, and also because for some reason he couldn't remember exactly how he'd planned it—except that he knew this wasn't it. Look at him: racing like a crazy man through the woods, like a maniac, all caution thrown to the wind. His legs were bleeding from brambles, his feet aching from the pounding they were taking, the muscles in his legs tightening up fast.

"I have to take it easy," Harry told himself desperately, but the words weren't out of his mouth before he was off again, legs driving like pistons and heart pumping, sweat rivering off his chin and down his neck, stinging between his legs and under his arms. His eyes were bugging now, partly from the unaccustomed straining, partly in horror of—of whatever it was—and his chest rose and fell ever faster, the air burning in his lungs. All of his exercising hadn't prepared him for this.

Then he saw the stream up ahead. Water. Dragonflies hummed like tiny helicopters over the cool water. He plunged on toward the stream, went down on his knees at the bank—but he didn't drink. In the mud there, something shiny. Harry reached out a hand—

It was like his brain had received an electric shock. He reeled and clapped his hands to his head, sucking air until the pain went away. Then, through eyes that were stinging and blurred, he looked again at the Hlitni spacecraft. A tiny dark patch grew on the silver, an opening. Something slender emerged and glinted in the sunlight. Harry snatched back his face instinctively, and that was the second last instinctive thing that he ever did.

A tiny projectile—trailing a wire so slender that the world's smallest spider might have difficulty spinning anything of a narrower gauge, yet strong enough to swing a brick—flashed up to strike Harry between the eyes, penetrating the bone. As he leaped to his feet with a cry of outrage and shock—the very last instinctive thing he ever did—the projectile rapidly reeled in its wire, at the end of which sat Sarl in his pinhead capsule. The whole thing took little over a second.

Harry staggered stiffly at the stream's edge for a moment, then stood stock still. In less than fifteen seconds as he stood there, his heart slowed down to normal, his respiration quieted down, his eyes stopped bugging and took on a peculiar glaze. Then he moved, wading slowly out through the stream, being especially careful to avoid the Hlitni ship, splashing for the far bank in water up to his knees. He stepped up onto the bank and tried out his arms, swinging them. He turned his head left and right, focused his eyes, drew air into his lungs until his chest swelled out.

Then he started to run again, slowly at first but picking up speed and coordination as he went. Harry "the Hit" Coggin was in gear, engine running —but Sarl sat at the steering wheel and it was Sarl's foot on the accelerator. The Hlitni had their vehicle . . .

V.

"He had me worried there for a moment," said Klee. "When he reached out to touch the ship."

"Yes," Inth answered. "With the power-cells drained he could easily have crushed us. It is fortunate that we didn't stun him when we all three pressured his mind together!"

Klee offered a mental nod, and this too was communicated to Inth. Then, after a moment's silence, he said: "I believe we are still sinking."

"*I was about to suggest,*" answered Inth, "*that we attract two of the small, four-winged flyers, just in case we have to evacuate. They scan out a very short life-cycle, but we could always transfer later if the need arose.*" And as an afterthought, he added: "*They are quite fast—could take us to Sarl in no time at all.*"

"*How's he getting on?*" Wondered Klee, using his magnet mind to snare a dragonfly and pull it, unresisting, to hover over the gradually settling vessel.

"*By now he should have mastered his vehicle completely,*" answered Inth. "*Let's see how he is doing, shall we?*"

Sarl was doing very well indeed. Harry's body functioned as never before, at maximum efficiency. Mindless, operating solely at Sarl's direction, he plunged through the final fringe of woodland to arrive at the edge of the fields beyond. In the distance smoke curled upward into the late afternoon sky from unseen cottages; skylarks sang in the still-blue sky; the bark of a dog at play carried on the still air from afar. Sarl noticed all of these things but immediately put them aside. This was no time for studying an alien world through alien eyes; there was barely sufficient time to get through with the job in hand. He sensed Inth and Klee the moment they scanned him.

"*How am I doing?*" he asked.

"*Dead on course.*" Inth answered

"*The power source is presently situated in that clump of trees on the hill up ahead,*" directed Klee.

"*Thanks for the confirmation,*" said Sarl gratefully. "*I was a fraction disorientated. He handles beautifully, but it's a bit difficult to control him and stay right on course at one and the same time.*"

"*Hey!*" Inth came in again. "*I scan a pair of bipeds in those trees. They are right beside the power source. Is that odd, I wonder?*" His mental voice, boosted by the communicators, frowned. "*I don't think I quite like . . .*" he paused, then quickly went on: *"And Sarl, you'll have to get moving faster. The ship's going down into the mud quite quickly now."*

VI.

Constables Williams and Brown had driven their white police car up a grassy incline to park it in a lone clump of trees bearding the southern slope of a hill. The hill stood between the nearest village and the woods proper, and under the cover of the trees they would be hidden from the view of Harry if he chose to make a break for it within their radius of responsibility. Such would be most unlikely, of course; the woods formed a front some miles long, of which each police sector was only a fraction.

There were eight more cars spread out about the woods; sixteen more constables in all, not to mention a smaller number of plainclothes men. Several of the latter detectives were armed; it was generally accepted that Harry "the Hit" Coggin wasn't going to come quietly. Still, and where constables Williams and Brown were concerned, the odds were about eight to one against him coming out of the woods just here. He certainly wouldn't do it in daylight . . .

Which was why Williams almost dropped his binoculars when, from out the fringe of the woods, plainly unabashed and in no way attempting to hide his presence, Harry Coggin ran into the late sunlight of the open fields. The fugitive stood for a moment, turning his head left and right, then seemed to gaze straight up the grassy slope of the hill at the spot where Williams stood with his binoculars, hidden in the shade of a tree. For a moment Williams stared directly into the other's eyes, and he couldn't help but notice, even through the glasses, how strangely vacant those orbs were.

"Well I'll be—" he excitedly whispered, passing the glasses to Brown who quickly put them to his eyes. "He's here!" Then, while Brown kept a close watch on Harry, Williams went to the car radio and quietly, urgently passed on the news.

Meanwhile, drawn as if by a magnet to the hidden police car, Harry came across a field and up the hill in an unerringly, unnaturally straight line. His clockwork legs drove him forward and up; his strange eyes were fixed unflinchingly upon the clump of trees near the hill's summit.

Brown, previously complacent, quickly became nervous. . . Still watching the rapidly approaching runaway, he said out of the corner of his mouth: "Ere, George. This bloke's supposed to be dangerous, ain't 'e? Look at the size of 'im. 'E's bleedin' . . . 'uge!"

"It's okay, Fred. There'll be some more of the blokes here in no time. They're on their way now."

"But 'e's supposed to be after a car, ain't 'e?"

"He'll probably run," Williams answered uncertainly, "as soon as he sees us." After a moment's thought he added: "Of course, we could always jump him. We can hide and hit him as soon as he pokes his head in here."

"Listen," Brown insisted. "I've 'eard about this bloke. 'E's not the kind you jump—'e's a killer, 'e is!" He immediately searched around and found himself a short, club-like branch of a fallen tree. Williams, feeling suddenly naked, did the same.

And on came Harry, veering from his immaculately straight course only to avoid obstacles in his path: a thick clump of gorse bushes, a boulder, a lone tree. And his speed was such that the blue-clad watchers in the trees knew he would surely reach them before the help they had called on the radio. The plan had gone sour. Harry "the Hit" Coggin had not waited for nightfall; he had not even attempted to remain under cover, out of sight. His approach was almost insolent, mechanical . . . it seemed to Williams and Brown that he knew exactly what he was about. But all they could do was hide and wait.

Then, from the direction of the village, the constables heard the welcome growl of a car's engine, and knew as soon as they saw its black bonnet nosing up through the grass of the hillside that it contained plainclothesmen, detectives who would probably be armed.

"Trap!" Inth's telepathic warning sounded sharp in Sarl's receptors. *"Those two bipeds in the trees are waiting for you, I'm sure of it!"*

"But what—? How—?" Sarl began.

"No time for questions and answers. Just concentrate on what you're doing," Klee came in. *"We need that power source. It's our one chance. You have your vehicle, Sarl, and it's a powerful one. It should make a powerful weapon, too. Use it!"*

VII.

When young, up-and-coming detective-inspector Rimbolt climbed out of his car, it was to be met with a scene of savagery. His driver, as young as himself and less experienced, was similarly awed. Constable Williams, his skull laid open to the bone, was writhing on the ground in the shade of the trees, shouting unintelligibly and moaning between shouts. Brown was in the act of battering Harry "the Hit" Coggin with the branch of a tree; Coggin held up his arms before him and deftly fended off the blows. Then Brown's club struck the fugitive's shoulder and there was an audible crack. The stricken shoulder slumped, but at the same time Coggin brought Brown a backhander that flattened the policeman's nose and hurled him down in the leaves and earth.

At that, with a shouted command, detective-inspector Rimbolt snatched out his police automatic and leveled it at the fugitive. Coggin took absolutely no notice but stooped, scooped up Brown's unconscious form, tossed it like a rag doll at the newly arrived pair. The two of them were knocked off their feet, Rimbolt's gun discharging harmlessly in the air.

As Rimbolt climbed to his feet there came the sound of rending metal. He could hardly believe the evidence of his own eyes. There stood Coggin, wrenching at the bonnet of the white police car, tearing it open with his bare hands—no, with his bare *hand*, for his right arm hung almost uselessly at his side.

Even as the wide-eyed detective watched, bolts sheared and metal creaked. Finally the dented, twisted bonnet flew up with a crash and Coggin leaned forward to tear at the car's heavy battery. Blood flew from fingers lacerated on sharp metal edges as he straightened, tucking the battery under his good arm.

Then the blue-clad form of Rimbolt's driver hurtled out from the shade of the trees, striking Coggin in a rugby tackle as the fugitive turned from the car. "Good man!" Rimbolt shouted, searching desperately for his fallen weapon. Then, as he found the gun and turned back to the scene at the car, there came a sickening crunch—and a brief gurgling sound.

Harry "the Hit" Coggin kneeled over the young policeman's body, holding the battery high in one huge hand. With brutal force he brought it down into the already crushed and bubbling pulp of the young man's face. Aghast, Rimbolt cocked his weapon and fired it at Coggin from a distance of no more than fifteen feet. He missed, squeezed the trigger a second time . . . Nothing happened, dirt had blocked the firing-pin.

—Then Coggin looked up and saw him.

Rimbolt froze. The look in the killer's eyes was indescribable: not madness, neither that nor hate, nothing like Rimbolt had ever seen before. He backed away from Coggin, stumbling backward through low shrubbery, his mouth open and dry, eyes wide in fear. Then the fugitive climbed lopsidedly to his feet, turned away and began to run. Back down the grassy slope toward the woods, he went, the battery tucked under his good arm, swaying and stumbling like a badly balanced robot.

Rimbolt's nerve returned. He quickly cleaned the firing-pin of his gun and kneeled against the bole of a tree. He aimed two-handed at the raggedly running figure and squeezed the trigger. The bullet hit Coggin somewhere low in the rear right of his body, probably his kidney, Rimbolt thought, spinning him through three hundred and sixty degrees. He fell, tumbling head over heels down a steeper part of the slope.

"Got you—you bloody black-hearted bastard!" Rimbolt shouted. Then his jaw dropped and he shook his head in utter disbelief. Coggin had climbed to his feet, was hobbling now with a queer, lurching gait, and still he carried the battery. Before the detective-inspector could take aim again the fugitive had disappeared into the trees.

VIII.

"*I'm in trouble!*" Sarl fearfully reported. "*Each part of this creature's anatomy seems to rely more or less on its neighboring parts—very much like the Gvries of Sapha-sapha VII. Right now parts of the system are trying to close down, the mind particularly. I've deadened the pain areas but that's had little effect. He's lost a lot of efficiency; he's losing blood, too, where he was shot . . . Leaking like a pitted power-cell.*"

"*Are you going to make it?*" Inth remained comparatively calm.

"*Oh, I'll make it—providing there are no more interruptions!*"

"*Yes,*" Inth told him, "*I was just about to mention that . . .* "

"*Eh?*"

"*Klee and I have been scanning the area where we first picked up your vehicle. There are a lot more of them closing in—bipeds like him. They have quadrupeds with them. Symbiotic, at a guess. It looks serious. After the reception you got when you went for the power source, we have to assume—*"

"*I'm not a complete Yhinn!*" Sarl heatedly protested, not waiting for Inth to finish. "*They saw us come in; they probably know what we're up to; they're trying to stop us!*"

"*You could very well be right, yes.*"

"*Can't you two throw them off, send them on a false trail?*"

"*We've already tried that,*" Klee came in, a little less calmly than Inth. "*After all, we're no more Yhinnish than you, Sarl—less Yhinnish, most of the time. The bipeds we could probably confuse a little, even though there are several of them, but the quadrupeds are particularly single-minded. They are tracking your vehicle and show only a passing interest in the illusions we've thrown at them. If we had more time, more experience of this world's life-forms—and if we knew exactly—"*

"*If, if, if!*" snapped Sarl, quite insubordinately. "*Forget it! Just maintain tracking contact with me, that's all. I've trouble enough without worrying about anything else. I'm doing my best to control a careening, damaged, barely functioning vehicle—and the trees in this wood all look alike to me!*"

"*Temper, Sarl!*" Inth snapped right back. "*How can you hope to control any vehicle when it's plain you can barely control yourself? Just make sure—*"

"*Trouble!*" came Klee's boosted warning, cutting off Inth's rebuke. "*There are two more bipeds hot on your trail, Sarl. They're closing with you fast. You'd better get that big vehicle of yours moving . . .*"

"*Do you want me to burn him out? He's badly damaged—and he's already going as fast as I can push him. Anyway, I'm nearly home. Be ready to take me aboard.*"

Plainclothesmen Carter and Dodds had witnessed at a distance some of the action atop the wooded hill, and they had tried to take steps to cut Coggin off if he made a run for the woods again. Possibly they would have been successful had their car not bogged down in marshy ground to one side of the hill.

They had not thought for a moment to climb the hill in the tracks of the other two cars; there were already four policemen up there, one of them armed, and Coggin was, after all, only one man. When their car got stuck fast they had scrambled out of it in time to see Coggin knocked down by Rimbolt's shot, his fantastic recovery, finally his hobbling escape into the trees. They had known something of the man's unenviable reputation, but nothing of his near-invincibility!

Immobilized by astonishment for a few seconds only, at last the detectives had set out after Coggin on foot, their weapons cocked and to hand. He had not been difficult to follow: where he'd passed, the ground and foli-

Brian Lumley

age were splashed with blood. He certainly wouldn't get far with a wound as bad as his must be.

Following the fugitive's scarlet trail—made doubly easy by the sounds of his crashing through the underbrush somewhere ahead—they moved as fast as they could. They were eager to put an end to this thing. Neither of them doubted for a single moment that the wounded man would surrender as soon as they had him cornered; his wound and their weapons permitted of no other possible conclusion. Suddenly Dodds caught his colleague's arm, dragging him to a halt.

"What's up?" Carter asked, his voice hushed in the wood's green shade.

"Listen . . . you hear anything? No? I think he's gone to ground. Either that or he's keeled over. Come on, let's get him!"

IX.

A minute later, entering an area of the wood where the boles of stout oaks towered high, as Carter ran past one such pillar, Sarl was waiting. He had his vehicle in gear and ticking over, with his foot on the clutch, and as Carter came into view he gunned Coggin's big motor and released the man's coiled muscles.

Right behind Carter, Dodds saw the massive, bloody fist strike out and clout the side of his colleague's head, knocking him clean off his feet with its force. Quite definitely Carter was out cold, if not dead, and now Coggin swung to face the second of his pursuers. For a split second Dodds looked into eyes that were utterly empty—then he squeezed the trigger of his gun and Coggin was blasted back, arms flung wide, into tangled briars.

Knowing he had hit the big man in his right breast and guessing quite reasonably that he had done for him, Dodds put his gun away, stepped forward and leaned over Coggin's spread-eagled body. The empty eyes flicked open and stared at him; the terrible left hand whipped up and grabbed his throat, pulling him down. Dodds made several ugly, gurgling sounds as his windpipe was crushed. Then the big hand left his throat, bunched into a knot and struck him like a hammer in the forehead. Finally his body was tossed aside and Coggin staggered upright. His hands, trunk and legs were covered in blood that pumped and splashed from his wounds. He swayed, awkwardly picked up the battery from where it lay nearby, then turned and moved on into the woods. Astride the man's dimly flickering brain Sarl grimly urged the last dregs of life out of his crippled, dying vehicle.

X.

"They have released one of the quadrupeds," Inth's message boosted into Sarl's mind. *"It's coming in this direction, and it's coming fast. It could be after you—after your vehicle—or it could be after us! There's no way of knowing. Controlling their bodies is a very different hash of khrumm to reading their alien minds. We have tried to get into this quadruped's mind, but no use. So you'd better hurry, Sarl, hurry!"*

"I'm here," Sarl answered, desperately fighting to keep Coggin's bloodied almost-corpse aloft, *"already at the stream—and I see the quadruped!"*

Bruce, a big black Alsation, always unruly and excitable, had slipped his leash when his handler stumbled on a root. That had been immediately after the party skirted the boggy area about the pond. With the quarry's scent strong in his nostrils and ignoring his master's commands, Bruce had bounded off into the trees and bushes. Apart from his unruliness, Bruce had one other problem: an unwillingness to let go until his target stopped moving! Once the target, or quarry, was down and disarmed, a police dog could usually be called off—but not Bruce. That was why his handler was sweating now as he raced through the woods after his runaway dog. If Bruce caught up with Coggin alone, he'd simply kill him out of hand!

Driven almost to a frenzy as Coggin's scent grew stronger, the dog had quickly covered the last mile. Now he broke from the cover of the trees onto the bank of the stream. Ears erect, nose eagerly sniffing the air, Bruce's dog eyes took stock of two separate items. A bright shiny thing lay low in the mud close to the bank, and across the narrow strip of water a man lurched drunkenly, almost falling as he splashed out into the stream. The shiny thing was immediately forgotten; Coggin's scent was so strong now that Bruce could almost taste it. With a whine of fury building to a snarl in his throat, he sprang to the attack.

Coggin's eyes were glazing, sending blurred pictures to Sarl. Nevertheless he saw the dog bounding across the stream toward him, saw the leap that brought the furry horror snarling for Coggin's throat. If Sarl's vehicle should be knocked off his feet now, the Hlitni driver knew he'd never get it up again. He directed all of Coggin's departing strength into his left arm and hand, swung the battery in a deadly arc. Brain and fur went flying as Bruce's final leap ended in crunching death.

As the dog's body went floating slowly downstream, Sarl pushed Coggin a few more paces forward, tossed the battery to land on the bank eight feet ahead of him, and said:

"For Great Hlita's sake . . . !"

The corpse went down on its knees in the water, swayed from side to side. The lights behind its eyes went out . . . and something flashed across the distance between the tiny spacecraft and Coggin's brow. A second later, as the corpse toppled forward, the rescue capsule was reeled in again and Sarl was back in the ship. Coggin lay face down in the stream, anchored by reeds, bobbing gently with the current, staining the water red.

Fifteen minutes later, as velvet evening started to settle and yellow lights in local village streets began to come on one by one, the spaceship's silver spike hovered over high tension cables where they stretched between great pylons. Briefly, causing no one the slightest concern, the lights in the villages dimmed and distant generators felt a momentary draining. Then the lights brightened again and curious observers might have noticed a tiny meteorite that traced a line of fire upward across the dusk of England. The Hlitni had departed, leaving behind a mystery that no man would ever solve satisfactorily.

The Vehicle

Out into the spaces between the stars they sped, hurdling the light years that separated them from their destination. And in its cocoon in the bowels of the ship their new vehicle lay cool and asleep and uncaring, hastily commandeered against some yet unseen future need, pollen of the flowers of Earth still clinging to its legs. When they awakened it, for however brief a time, it would serve them no more complainingly than had Harry "the Hit" Coggin, and . . . who knows? Perhaps, when they had replaced it with a vehicle more to their liking, it would then go on to buzz out its lifespan exploring the strange flowers of some alien world's warm jungles.

Perhaps one day, Hybrid blooms would burn beyond Orion . . .

THANKS
Elizabeth Massie

WINTER ARRIVED, AND WITH IT THE SCENTS AND SOUNDS of the holidays. Snow covered the fields with sparkling white. The sky was cloudless and as blue as a periwinkle. The breath of the thick-coated cattle rose heavily into the air, like wood smoke curling from a farmhouse chimney. Our footsteps crunched the frozen ground as we did our early morning chores.

Ruth and I are twins, and at sixteen, are the oldest of the children. This year we were excited, barely able to contain ourselves. Two of the grown-up chores had been passed from our father to us. One was to chop the family's Christmas tree. The other was to bring in the Blue Ridge oysters for the Christmas feast.

Finding a tree was easy. Seven-year-old Jenni had picked it out in August when we'd been gathering blueberries on the ridge beyond our barn. A fine blue spruce it was, tall and straight with needles smelling of tart-sweet sap. Ruth and I took turns with the axe and felled it with four strokes. We dragged it back to the house in the snow and by the time we got there, it was dusted with ice. Jenni said it looked like a jewel tree, and was sad when we put it up in the parlor and the ice melted in the heat of the woodstove. But Mama got out the box of ornaments and the tears didn't last.

The oysters were another matter. Ruth and I had brought them in with Daddy for a couple years and we both knew it took skill and patience. When Daddy handed us the knives this year, he had winked and said, "Watch you don't get kicked!"

I nodded. Last year, Daddy had gotten kicked really hard in the shin and spilled the basket into the creek. Most of the oysters had washed away before we could grab at them with our wet and soggy wool gloves. Mama had been furious, because without the oysters, she said, Christmas dinner wasn't complete. We'd given thanks, but I'd heard the disappointment in Mama's prayer.

"We'll be careful," Ruth told Daddy. And off we went, up behind the barn, over the ridge, and into the pine forests that stretched beyond it.

The first four were not hard at all, much to our delight. Surprise had given us the advantage, and we'd sung snippets of Christmas carols as we'd dropped the fat, tasty morsels into our collecting basket. It was best to get these delicacies free-range, Daddy had always told us. Not that it affected quality, but it sure did affect the ease with which they were collected.

But it got dark before we had gathered enough, and Ruth talked me into sneaking into an unfamiliar barnyard and hiding in a stall so we could get at least two more. I was apprehensive; Daddy had always said there was danger in close quarters. Ruth shook her head and said I worried too much. "We're young, fast, and strong!" she whispered. And so we crouched and held still, waiting.

It was not fifteen minutes before we heard him snorting and snuffling in the aisle. Ruth raised her knife. It threw back dull bits of winter light. She grinned at me. I lifted my knife, and we jumped out of the stall.

He bellowed and fell with a crash to the manure-covered floor as Ruth and I landed on him. Ruth wedged her knees and elbows in, keeping him as still as she could as I went to work with my knife. He bucked and twisted, but years of watching Daddy had taught me the necessity of accuracy. Four strokes, easy and smooth like those with the tree, and I had the prize.

"Let him up!" I shouted.

We jumped and ran. We didn't stop until we were in the forest where I'd left the basket. I dropped the oysters in, and only then did I double over to cough and laugh.

And we laughed until our sides hurt. "That was the easiest one yet," I managed. "I think he had a girl in the barn. He didn't have any pants on!"

We laughed again. And then we took the basket home in the dark, proud of our collection, knowing this year Mama would give cheerful thanks for yet another feast.

THE GALVANIC
James S. Dorr

"YE MAY SAY THAT BANKERS HAVE HEARTS OF FLINT," Dr. N_____ pro-claimed—I will not say what his name was here, though you would recognize it if you saw it— "or likewise men of the legal professions, but I will tell you that there are none so hard and unyielding as those of our own Edinburgh physicians."

We strained to hear him, my fellow neophytes and I, as we waited in the dimly lit chamber above Surgeons' Hall for what was to be our first full-body anatomy session. The gas jets' hiss vied with his words for our instructor was quite into his years, so old in fact that he himself had studied under the notorious Dr. Knox, and, prior to that, both Drs. Monro, *secundus et tertius*. His voice thus could rise to little more than a whisper, but he whose work on *The Branchings of the Human Nerve System* is still read today, continued to perform demonstrations as his health permitted. And even when not he remained with the College, as he did this night, if not to deliver the lecture from the platform behind the cadaver himself, then at least to wield the exemplary pointer.

Oh, his hands were still steady, if his voice was not—more steady that night than those of some of our own young students, I would dare say myself. One of our fellows had already fainted, in anticipation, and more than one looked a bit green at the jowls. But the old man went on.

"Let me tell you," he said, "of the corpse you will be seeing cut open soon. But before even that, let me tell you a story . . . "

•   •   •

In days some time back (the aged surgeon said), before the Warburton Anatomy Act was finally passed in '32 which thus allowed subjects for lectures as this night's to be come by legally, there were men—often of dubious honesty — who had to be dealt with, known variously as "Resurrectionists" or "Sack-'em-up Men." These were the ones who supplied the bodies for Schools such as this one, as well as the various private lectures most physicians offered.

The money was good, you see, for their labors. Cadavers were needed—they had to be gotten—and therefore could command prices of thirty or forty pounds or more to those that dug them up. More than enough to provide a living for men with little of education and still less of morals, even when out of the take would come bribes for churchyard sextons, and guards and others, to find different places to cast their eye when the digging and sacking were going on.

So it was too, though, that some cut corners—the Burkes and Hares of our fair city, the Bishops and Mays of London, and others—and some of the corpses received were, to put a delicate point to it, overly fresh. And others were stolen from fellow Sack-'em-ups, often from Ireland and shipped to our own shores. Gangs roamed the streets for that, robbers of robbers, and not averse to "Burking" their own fellows should the opportunity come for it, requiring only that first there be liquor sufficient to quiet the intended victim in order that the corpse be procured without marks of violence.

Oh, those were shameful days, made all the worse by the rivalries among our own physicians—stealing students one from the other to increase their own fees as well as their learning. But as one's number of students grew larger, so too did the need for more bodies in order to support yet more lectures. And so the cycle grew, feeding upon itself. Corpses were often mailed in from the countryside by rural constables, seeking to turn a profit from other people's misfortunes. Bodies from hospitals sometimes were "mislaid" before they could be claimed by grieving relations. And we, the physicians, the doctors and students, did nothing to stop this. We *needed* cadavers. One cannot bring an ill person to health unless one has first learned the body's workings, how flesh and muscle and bone and sinew are put together, how nerves and blood vessels bring spark and nutrition to all fleshly parts, that the whole might enjoy life. And thus we, life's saviors or so we would hope to be, given enough learning and enough skill, contributed most in our own at-all-costs-avoid-questioning-too-deeply-whence-subjects-came way to what had become the mockery of death's peace.

And then, Burke and Hare. As I said before, though others preceded them, the need for bodies became so great that some did not even go to the churchyard, but rather selected the poor, the friendless, the widowed, the lonely, the all-but-forgotten shadows of humankind, lost in its corners — or so they thought!—and did them in on the very streets! And all for the rapaciousness of we, the doctors.

Of course they were needed. The bodies, that is. Science could not advance without them, both for demonstrations for learning, and for other matters. And so too were the Sack-'em-ups needed in increasing numbers, the latter of course to supply of the former.

But when the ghastly art turned to murder . . . ah, that's when the outcry went up of "foul!" Bad enough to rob graves, and now the public had roused itself up against the ghouls. And against the ghouls' employers as well.

Knox, who in innocence had but received a fresh-murdered body, found his career ruined. His house nearly burned down. And yet, for us others, by now there was no stopping receiving corpses, whatever their provenance, lest their suppliers should peach on *us* and we be ruined too.

Thus was the winter of 1830, a year after Burke's hanging and, by the irony of the law at that time, anatomizing by Monro *tertius* in public session as warning to others who might perform murder. I had of course left Dr. Knox by then—to have done otherwise would have been unsafe—sojourning on the Continent some while with Prof. F_____ and Dr. T_____. And so, when I returned to Scotland intending to start my own surgical practice, I found conditions somewhat changed.

Oh, the old rivalries among physicians still continued, if anything fiercer than when I had left, but the Resurrectionists' ways had evolved as they, too, had been forced to take a lower profile. Needing cadavers, I found an Irishman who could provide them. But as that winter proceeded on to spring, all of a sudden, as these things would happen from time to time, the supply dwindled.

I could not find other Sack-'em-up Men to augment this supply without incurring the wrath of the man I was already in with. Such was the power these men had over us—blackmailers, really, as they turned out to be—that it was almost as if we did *their* bidding than they did ours. And so my Irishman, when I accosted him about the necessity of getting new corpses, put this somewhat peculiar proposition to me:

"Guv'nor," he said, "I do have this one body, and it shall be yours as soon as it's ready. And I can get others on similar terms. But ye must pay first. Ye get me drift on this?"

I shook my head. "No." I did not get his drift, yet.

He explained himself further. "The body is *mine*. As ye see, I'm in ill health—I shan't have much time left in any event so I may as well spend me last months in comfort." He coughed as if to underscore his point, but I believed him. The work at night. The digging of corpses, some that had passed away of diseases. Not to mention the wrath of the mob that still persisted, making it dangerous for one to be seen on the city's streets at night with just so much as a pick or a shovel. All these conspired to make Resurrection work, at the least, an unhealthy trade.

"But," I protested, "I need a cadaver now. Whether yours or not—and, yes, I see now your hand's palsied shaking and have no doubt of its readiness soon—it must be in my chambers by tomorrow."

"Yes," said my Irishman. "I understand that. But, as I grow frail in my labor, so too has my sister who, as luck would have it, passed on just this evening. She had no friends, Guv'nor. I've told no one of it. And so I suggest to ye that if ye buy my corse on promise, to use as it's ready, I'll sell ye hers also."

What choice had I then? To buy an option on this man's own corpse struck me as foolish. Should he renege later, what recourse would there be? Surely not that of law! And, as I discovered the following winter when, as if by a miracle, his health had come back sufficiently for him to force me to buy a renewal on it, I was more than foolish. And yet, whether it be that of his sister, or of some poor streetwalker he'd had his eye on intending a Burking, I did need a body. And I needed it quickly.

And so, God help me, I took up his offer.

·   ·   ·

Dr. N_____ paused then and signaled one of us to bring him down a pitcher of water. While we waited, I thought I could hear the creak of a door downstairs, and then a faint whirring. The opening, possibly, of a back entrance to the hall, as well, who knows?, as the buzz of flies maybe. The night was quite warm and even though, under the present law, paupers' bodies could be got from hospitals provided no relatives stood in objection—and that they be given good Christian burial when they were done with—sometimes they would still not be quite of the freshest. And then the faint sound of a gasp—a shriek, maybe.

But by then Dr. N_____ had received his water and, confirming that the lecture would indeed be starting shortly, he placed the emptied glass back on its tray and continued his story.

◆ ◆ ◆

Was this Irishman a Burker? A murderer as well as a robber of church-yards? I have little doubt he was. You see, among doctors, though rivals we were, it was quite difficult for such things to be kept a secret. Our rivalry itself was the cause—we eagerly stole students from one another, passing them back and forth just as first one, then another of us would gain reputation for some new technique or experimentation. And so I had my share of others' students, as they had of mine, and these students brought gossip. Including gossip about this man who supplied to others as well as to me.

But that does not matter, concerning my story. What does is this: That my Irishman had become too greedy. I heard the gossip and soon ascertained that I was not the only surgeon who had paid him well, and continued to pay, for the promise of the use of his own body.

And so I called truce among us surgeons, discussing this, my new found knowledge, first with Dr. B_____ the Elder, then with the others, and confirmed that all, or nearly all, of the prominent surgeons of Edinburgh had paid this man for his corpse after death. Indeed, some had paid him for many years for it.

Now when our meeting occurred was in late spring, and then, as now, the Schools closed down from May to October. Thus we determined a confrontation, having no fear of repercussion—at least in terms of his refusing to supply us further should we press him too far—in that we still should have plenty of time to find new sources for the next session. We queried our students and, sure enough, there were several who had an idea of where our man resided. And so one evening the first week of May we marched to the poorer section of town, a fair mob ourselves of torch-bearing doctors, to have it out with him.

What we would have done with him I do not know, except he was fore-warned and, seeing our approach from his windows, determined to flee. He lit out a back gate of his tenement and, with us nearly upon his heels, coursed down winding streets and cobble-stoned alleys, often in darkness or nearly in darkness. So the pursuit went, a mile or more, with all the time a fog starting to rise up out of the Firth, when, all of a sudden, he dodged out into the lights of a wide square and directly into the path of a carriage.

The driver pulled his horses up as best he could, but already it was too late to avoid him. We, as doctors, of course took the body that even though most terribly trampled, still had some spark of life left within it. We took him to Surgeons' Square and to this very building here and, such was our oath, we did the best we knew how to save him. To save his worthless life which before—who knows what we might have done in our anger? And yet . . .

           ✦   ✦   ✦

Dr. N_____ paused again to take more water. His voice had been fail-ing, and yet we'd been listening with such rapt attention I doubt a one of us had missed a single word. In the silence we heard the gas jets and, under-neath, in the hall below, the sounds of rustling. Of surgical instruments be-ing made ready. A soft keening sound like the grunt of a workman, perhaps in his straining to move the table the subject of the night would be laid on.

And then, the strength of his voice renewed somewhat, the old man continued.

           ✦   ✦   ✦

God help me, I say. We are all of us God-fearing men in this room, I think. Learning the wonder of God's creation, the image of God laid out in Man's body, despite what some of the Rationalists say can only serve to strengthen our Faith, not to cause it to falter. And yet, as we struggled to save this poor man's life, despite the grievance we justly had of him, I saw the looks of my fellow doctors. I saw how they glanced as the spark of life faded, then finally snuffed out, as if it were pity his corpse had been trampled and so, unless the tedious work of repairing its damage be somehow accomplished before it go bad, was of no use to them.

And, moreover, it was nearly summer . . .

At last first one, and then another, gave up the task. Dr. M_____ signed the death certificate, then singly and in pairs they departed, some of them murmuring that, at the end, the Irishman had at least saved them the problem of which, of the many he had sold himself to, would be able to lay claim upon him.

But I, I had studied in France as I say, and also Vienna. I had studied under T_____ and F_____ who, in their own turn, had been disciples of the celebrated Franz Anton Mesmer. I had a grounding, rare for a Scottish surgeon at that time, in the theories of Galvani, that animal life was the cause of electromagnetic force, and of their refutation by Volta. And I had, myself, formulated my own thoughts.

Thus, alone with this newly-dead subject, unable to save him by other means, I now determined to try these out. I called for servants, had them bring me Voltaic cells, a large tub of water, and salts and powders and coils of copper wire. Into the tub I placed the Irishman, fixing the coils to his hands and feet, and started the current. I fully expected his feet to kick, as Galvani's frogs' legs did, a mere reaction as Volta had proved to the force that flowed into them from the charged cells. But I also expected, as Mesmer had, that there might be more to it, that Volta as well had not seen the whole picture. And so I proved that night.

I never did publish the whole that I learned. And that for good reason. But Volta was wrong in not following up his work's conclusions. That, yes, it was true that animal life was not the creator of electrical forces, but—and this he failed to see—quite the opposite thing *was* the case. That Galvani, after all, had been the farther along the correct track.

That, properly applied to a subject, electrical force was the cause of life.

♦　　♦　　♦

"But why?" one of we students interrupted as our aged instructor once more briefly paused. "That is, you say you still did *not* publish . . . ?"

And then we heard again the odd buzzing noise from the hall below us, but louder this time and surely not of flies. Rather of some kind of apparatus. *And with it a loud scream!*

The old man nodded.

♦　　♦　　♦

I'm almost finished (he assured us) but *there* is your answer. It lies in the pain. I brought the Irishman back to life, but the first thing he did when I did so was howl in anguish. The current coursing through his body—it must have hurt dreadfully. And yet I kept it on, modulating it, turning it down to a tiny trickle—his cries to a low moan—but never having quite the courage to shut it entirely off. Rather I called back my fellow surgeons, having servants rouse them from their homes, from their very beds, to see this miracle I had accomplished. They, as I, agreed that unless I find some way to prevent the unimaginable suffering that this treatment necessarily brought with it, I should not publish a word of my findings. But also they agreed, even though the certificate be signed, that in that I had restored the corpse to life, it would be a violation of our solemn oath as physicians should any one of us endeavor to end it.

And yet . . . and I ask you now to remember what I said of flint hearts when I began this. And bankers and those of the legal professions.

For one of our number recalled the contracts. The contracts that each and every one of us had in possession, signed by this man's hand, willing to each the use of his corpse upon death for anatomical demonstration.

And, further, that Dr. M_____ *had* signed the death writ.

And yes—*you hear him now!*—that selfsame Irishman, that *Galvanic*, that resurrected-himself-Resurrectionist, his still living cadaver long since repaired of its trampling, laid on the table below in the Hall awaiting our presence. We will get him drunk first, before we cut him, to deaden not so much the agony of his dissection, but rather to quiet him lest his continuing shrieks otherwise interrupt the lecture. And then, once more, we shall repair him of any damage—and some of the brighter of you may help us—for he will be used again and again, as he has before, waiting the time between each year's new lecture, each new group of students, within his tub in the building's basement, the current turned down as much as we dare. But still with him always.

And so you have now a lesson of surgeons, what you will become yourselves. And you know now of their minds that can match wits with barristers' when it comes to enforcing contracts. And hearts of flint as stone-hard as bankers' in calculating the compounds of interest and drawing out worth to its final penny.

But there is another thing too you have learned now: A surgeon's faith in God. And in the life God grants to each of us, through whatever means, and the alternative lest you should think that keeping this man in pain as we do for repeated cuttings might tinge of cruelness.

He did, after all, sign a number of contracts, which to break would violate God's law as well as Scotland's; and, for all we know, he may also have at times committed murder. We do know he was a cheat, and a blackmailer. We know thus something of his soul's condition, you see, and what would become of it should we release it.

And that is the crux. We argued it, yes, throughout that whole summer, I often as not saying *"No! Let him die now!"* But I at last, also, was brought to consensus:

That this is our oath, as God is my witness, to heal the sick—to bring the ill comfort in soul as in body. To pass on this teaching even as we are about to commence in the chamber below a few moments henceforth.

And, thus, what we do is an act of mercy.

SHEETS
Donald R. Burleson

THE ROOM WAS PILED WAIST-HIGH WITH DRIFTED SNOW. Or so she thought for a moment, standing at a loss in the gray gloom of the parlor. Why had she come in here? She seldom entered this room. Did she? Strange, that she couldn't remember. The real snow would be at the windows soon enough, with the advent of winter, the brittle-cold death of the year that would bring a muffled quiet too much like the tomb. But for now the drifts of snow, gathered here incongruously in the room with her, were bedsheets: pale, lumpy shrouds covering a recumbent host of cadavers.

"Rebecca Hudson Payne," she said to the silence of the room, "you old fool. What in the world do you need in this room?" As if sensing themselves unimplicated in the question, the troupe of hunch-shouldered cadavers made no response.

They were, of course, nothing more than old furniture: a fossil table and chairs, two prehistoric sofas, an antediluvian coffeetable, various endtables predating all memory. Well, predating almost all memory, these ancient, dimly recalled relics from the time when Jonathan was alive.

The evil that men do . . .

It was an unbidden and unwelcome thought, stirring like a grub in her mind. She pushed it away, covered it with more wholesome thoughts, rather like pulling a bedsheet over old furniture that one would prefer no longer to behold. Trailing her faded nightgown, she stepped back across the worn and musty carpet and through the door to her bedroom, still wondering why she had entered the parlor in the first place, when everything about it made her uncomfortable.

◆　　　◆　　　◆

The kitchen window over the sink looked out across the leafless remains of the orchard, where gnarled branches of fruit trees clutched purposelessly at a cold Vermont sky the color of slate. From over the horizon, frothy clouds ran up like dirty dishwater, choking out what little suggestion remained of sunlight. She thought she heard something on the roof like tentative first hints of sleet, or was it just the wind, or birds? Her hearing wasn't what it once was, nor was her eyesight. It wasn't fair, this retreating of the senses, at a time in life when one felt one needed them most. Sometimes she felt helpless, a frightened animal in a hole. If it weren't for that delivery boy from the market bringing her groceries every week, how could she manage? Thank Heaven the house was long since paid for. Jonathan, at least, had seen to such things as that, though he'd never missed a chance to remind her of her dependence on him.

Without me, you'd be in the poorhouse, little Miss Hudson. He had loved to call her Miss Hudson, as if the most grindingly belittling thing he could say to her were to deny her the status of being married to him. *I pay all the bills around here*, he would add. That was the good side of him, if one could imagine a good side: he did pay the bills. Faithfully, scrupulously, with a kind of disdain for anyone who would do less.

The evil that men do lives on after them; the good is oft interred with their bones . . .

Odd, that she could remember her Shakespeare when she could no longer remember more immediate things. Was the house, then, if it represented his interred *good*, even more of a tomb than it seemed? She resisted the thought. It might be lonely here, and almost morbidly quiet, but then had living with Jonathan Payne been better than being alone? She scarcely thought so.

I'm afraid of him, Mama . . .

Madelyn. That was the trouble with children, they never came to see you when they were immersed in their own faraway lives. Madelyn must be—how old now? Rebecca tried to think. Jonathan had been gone eleven years. What year—the calendar on the side of the refrigerator—good heavens, could that be possible, could Madelyn be fifty-two?

Fifty-two and never married.

Unlike her younger brother Michael, who had children of his own in college now. But what good was it for her to have grandchildren, and soon great-grandchildren, no doubt—unimaginably distant little creatures whose faces were indistinct ghosts, misty half-imagined faces never seen.

Somehow, during these ruminations, she had made her slow way across the kitchen and into her bedroom and through the door into the parlor, without realizing where she was going, and once again she stood disoriented among pallid gray-white shapes in the gloomy interior, the eternally chilly room, disused and dead.

The room where Jonathan had died. And where—but no, she wouldn't think about that.

Such a little wash of sunlight made its feeble way in here that until she touched the light switch just inside the door, the humped and shrouded forms around her were things more felt than seen, and when the light came on, a crowd of shadows shuddered and retreated, but did not vanish altogether. Rather, they clustered, conspiratorial, in corners, massing behind white-sheeted shapes, mystery behind mystery. She peered around her at the silent sheets, and heard the wind rise suddenly and sharply, a sad little chorus of moaning at the windowpanes, and she felt the subtle pain again in her right forearm, the little ache she always felt when a cold front came in. It was a sardonic old friend, almost, this pain, still with her at times after all these years, reminding her that if nothing else she was still alive to feel it.

Without warning, the vision sprang before her eyes, the image of his face that night so many years ago, ruddy and belligerent at the door. Even now she could almost fancy she smelled the sour breath of whiskey blown in her face, could almost feel once again the familiar panic clutching her chest as he pushed through the screen door and she scrambled to stay out of his way. His mood would grow uglier as the night wore on, and the rest had been inevitable at some point, she supposed, clutching the forearm now, letting the pain subside. The bone had never set quite right.

She stood for some time in the parlor, until night came on and the cheerless windows admitted only gaping squares of darkness. Later, back in the kitchen, she heated her milk on the stove and tried not to remember.

♦   ♦   ♦

But coming into the parlor always seemed to make her remember, and now she stood here chiding herself, again, for dwelling upon things that bothered her. At least daylight sometimes made the memories seem more distant, but again today—was it only last night that she was here?—again the day beyond the windowpanes grew sullen with clouds until the sky was like a great iron lid on the world, shutting out the warmth of the sun, and her mood darkened as if it were itself covered by clouds, or shrouded by dusty bedsheets. Maybe the comparison made sense, she thought, maybe my mind has come to be so much old furniture best put to rest.

Nonsense, she retorted: just because that's the way he made you feel, like—

Like a roach under my shoe, he snarled from somewhere inside her head. *That's about how much good you are to me most of the time, you know that?* His face would curl up into the usual sneer. *A little roach to step on.*

And he'd done his best to step on her, too, or step on her spirit anyway. The worst was the defiance, hurled like so much foulness at her, after she found out what had been happening. *So you know what you know. Don't do you no good, does it? You tell, and you know what'll happen.* He spoke to her now just as surely as if he stood there in the flesh.

Incredibly, after all these years, a hot tear brimmed over and found a path down her cheek when she thought of the outrage of it all.

I didn't want to do it, Mama. A thirteen-year-old face rose in her mind like a miserable phantom. *He said if I didn't—*

Damn him, damn him to hell, she thought, wiping at her face with the back of her hand and feeling the ache creep back into her arm. And damn the rest of them for never understanding. How many times altogether had he—? She knew what they all must have thought when she turned from his gravesite and walked away without tears, without looking back. They thought she was ungrateful, cold, uncaring, unreasonable. People never saw a marriage from the inside, so what did they know? Madelyn knew, oh yes, but she, like Rebecca herself, had been afraid, and for good reason. Madelyn had come home for the funeral and had cried, and it was almost funny to reflect that no one else understood what those tears were really about.

The wind pressed a mouthful of cold breath onto the windowpanes; the bedsheets, huddled around her in a clumsy circle, seemed to lift slightly, but it must only have been the uncertain light, for the room was perfectly still now, except for her own ragged breath. It wasn't good for her, being in here, and she wasn't coming in here anymore. Ever.

◆　　　◆　　　◆

But she did. The next day, or the day after that; it was hard to remember how much time had passed. Or to remember why she had come. She thought it had to do with something she had been thinking about, out in the kitchen, watching the bare branches of the fruit trees in the orchard bend and writhe in the gathering wind, a wind that brought petulant little suggestions of sleet to tap at the windows. Now she remembered.

Sheets

As much as she had resisted the idea before, she thought now that if she uncovered some of the furniture and looked at it, she might dispel some of the memories that nagged at her, might find that in seeing *his* furniture again for what it was, simply a dusty and half-forgotten collection of old chairs and sofas and tables, she could stop being haunted by him, could dismiss him as easily as she could dismiss his unsightly, tasteless furniture, items that he and he alone had chosen, purchased, brought home. She had to gaze at it all now with the contempt that it deserved, and that he deserved. She had to be rid of the thought of him, because at times his memory reared itself with such force in her mind that she half thought she could feel it, palpable and breathing, in the air about her, as if he had never really left the house altogether. She remembered his habits all too well. In his sick mind he would often lie in wait for her, bide his time until the right moment, and step suddenly up from behind her with some reproach that left her trembling, if not bruised. To this day she cringed when the floorboards creaked by themselves, because she half thought, for a moment, that it was Jonathan. It was as if something of him still lived in the house. That was a tragic thought, and she had to banish it from her mind.

Well, his wretched furniture was what was left of him, for pity's sake, all that was left, and she would lift the sheets and look at it and know, finally, how foolish it all was, how truly dead and gone *he* was.

But when she took the corner of one pale bedsheet in her hand, one sheet covering a long, lumpy surface that could only have been a sofa, she found that she couldn't do it. Somehow, she couldn't lift the corner of the sheet to peer at the sofa, for as she started to do so, a sense of loathing overwhelmed her, and she dropped the sheet from her twitching hand and left the room. It was as if she had been about to look squarely into the face of evil itself, and she just couldn't bring herself to do that.

· · ·

The winter came slowly, relentlessly on with its short days gray and somber and devoid of warmth, until spatterings of snow were assaulting the windowpanes and the wind sounded like a dirge. God in Heaven, why did no one ever come to see her, to cheer her up? Michael didn't live too far away to come, at least once in a while, but he probably hadn't been here half a dozen times since that day (four or five years ago, it must have been) when he had come in his truck to carry away—whatever it had been, she couldn't remember. Certainly, he had his wife and his children, but one would think that he could find time occasionally. Something about the thought of him disturbed her, now, and not just his failure to come visiting. Something else.

She found herself standing in the parlor again, with the sky growing opaque with snow beyond the windows and the wind playing among the angles of the house like the stops of some strange flute. The only other sound was the distant grumble of the furnace, down in the cellar, a dinosaur pushing its warm breath through the ducts, through the house. What was it that she couldn't quite—but a gust of wind interrupted her thought, and the lights went out.

She stood still in the dark, scarcely breathing, just listening, though she could not have said why. Around her the lightless room was perfectly silent.

Around her, she knew, the sheet-covered furniture stood in the dark like a company of quiet, patient goblins.

A sudden sense of blind panic seized her. Turning toward the door to the bedroom, she ran her arm into the door jamb and a sliver of pain ran through the old wound, and she found herself crying and feeling her way back out of the parlor and into the bedroom and then the kitchen, and fumbled in the cupboard for candles. When she finally had one lit, she sat at the kitchen table in the near-dark and calmed herself and watched the candle in its saucer in the middle of the table casting grotesque, jittering shadows around the room, and she tried to think what to do. The lights, the electricity—a power line was probably down somewhere, and she could do nothing about that. Maybe they'd get it fixed, but sometimes, she knew, it took many hours, or even days.

Meanwhile, the furnace had shut off, she realized now, and she hoped that the house would hold its warmth long enough for the power to come back on. Perhaps she only imagined that it was already getting colder in here, but in any case she got up and started moving about, to keep herself occupied and to keep warm. She fussed over the dishes, taking silverware from the drainer and putting it away in the drawer. She rummaged aimlessly among shadowy piles of papers and old magazines. She looked out the window into the night, where unseen trees must be muffling up in gray, dead snow. And at some point she found herself back in the parlor, holding her candle and looking about at the humpback silhouettes of the bedsheets, which seemed, in a surreal and unsettling way, to waver and shift in the candlelight.

The evil that men do lives after them . . .

Could some essence of a person still—

A blast of winter wind shook the windows in their sills, and as if her own frame had been shaken too she suddenly remembered.

Remembered what it was that Michael had carried away, that time, in his truck.

You don't use the stuff, Mama, and it just reminds you of—well, what I mean is, you don't need the stuff, and you don't like having it around, and Jenny and I could use it.

She had offered up no argument to that, but then it meant that nothing had been left on the parlor floor in here but the sheets that had covered Jonathan's furniture. It could only have been the ravages of age, these past years, that confused her enough to make her think that the sofas and chairs and tables were still under there.

And if they weren't, what *was*?

She had, in any event, little time to ponder the question, because now the movement in the room was not just an effect of the flickering candle. Merciful Heaven, a man's evil really could live after him, could linger and grow and take shape—many shapes—and the most frightening thing was not that the sheets were beginning to slip aside and down, so that what was under them, emerging, could gather more closely around her. The most frightening thing was not even that the humped and dusky forms, phlegmatic and unyielding, were offering her no way out of the room.

No, the most frightening thing of all was the thought of how very long and how very quietly they had waited.

WATER AND THE SPIRIT
Brian McNaughton

THEIR HORSES WADING DAINTILY IN MORNING MIST, Heinrich von der Hiedlerheim and his mighty men jingled down from their tall abode through a wood where autumn raged. This season of bright colors and luminous haze filled Heinrich to bursting with restlessness, an atavistic compulsion to follow the geese, or perhaps the mammoths, to seek the sun or sack Rome. His singers, his cup-bearers and his concubines were forced to work long hours in the autumn. His warriors worked even harder at avoiding playful combats that could tumble into wrathful sincerity.

"Know, O Prince!" The speaker burst upon them like a great fungus sprung up in their path. Men cursed, horses reared and shrieked, swords and axes flashed. Bristling with hair and twigs, brandishing a crooked cross of sticks, the apparition howled: "Know, O Prince, that Babylon's doom is upon you, for you have fornicated under every green tree. Woe unto him that riseth up early in the morning to follow strong drink! Woe unto him that would slay his brother to lie with his brother's wife! Woe unto him that would burn Jews on the Sabbath, eat meat on Friday and take the name of the Lord in vain!"

"Not every green tree," Heinrich protested.

"Aye, mock me with your pride! A sin! Your gluttony at table, your sloth in the service of Christ, your envy of your emperor, your lust for what creature so ever on two legs or four tempts you with its youth and warmth! Sins, sins, sins!"

"You have failed to task me with the sin of anger, but it tempts me. To remove this temptation and make you a forgiving Christian, I command my men to baptize you in yonder river."

"My lord, this is Holy Hugo," protested Reinhardt, who had earned himself a womanish name by sparing Magyar infants and dogs. But Lothar and Wolfgang were haply at the graf's right hand, and they sprang to seize the hermit by arms and legs. They swung him, lustily chanting the baptismal formula— " . . . et-spiritus sancti-amen!" —and lofted him out over the steely flood of the Edelwesel. Flapping and twisting like a shot crow, shrieking garbled maledictions, he fell into the torrent and sank.

Reinhardt said: "My lord, Holy Hugo—"

"Cannot, it would seem, walk on water."

"True. But he may be able to breathe it. Despite the apparent theological inconsistency, he is an infamous wizard."

♦   ♦   ♦

The warlord's most irksome neighbor, the Bishop of Wurzendorf, had recently imported Greekish artisans to build him a steam-bath. Upon arriving at the palace, Heinrich was told that the bishop, with his sweating acolytes and catamites, would receive him in that dissolute swamp. Heinrich was in the habit of bathing only when necessary, and of stripping naked only in darkness. But he suspected that the bishop knew this and was trying to put him off balance, so he braved it out.

"Your scars are a map of German triumphs!" the bishop cried in a voice that rose from an oily baritone to a jarring squeak. He was only fourteen, but neither his youth nor the stigma of bastardy had prevented him from earning a miter on the strength of his piety alone, as his uncle, Emperor Otto II, often boasted.

The only map that concerned Heinrich was that of his estates, upon which the prelate had grossly infringed, but it would be unwise to state his grievance at the outset. Better to confess some minor lapse and put the pudgy youth in a forgiving mood.

"My Lord Bishop, I have sinned," he said as he squeezed into the intolerably dense atmosphere and picked his way through a serpent's nest of invisible limbs. The bishop led him to an open cubicle and urged him to sit by his side on an oaken bench.

"You aren't going to start that, are you? 'Forgive me for this, forgive me for that.' Christ! It's enough to make me vomit, the things you folk get up to. I'm off duty now, dear graf, so wait until you see some paltering priest before you start babbling about what you do when you think of Our Blessed Mother."

Heinrich pressed on: "I slew the hermit known as Holy Hugo."

"Well, good for you!" The bishop clapped him on a stony shoulder, his velvety hand lingering for an instant longer than the warlord liked. "Eremites are supposed to report to me, you know. We can't have people going off into the wilderness and praying by themselves, can we? Holy Hugo never reported, and anyone I sent to remind him never came back."

"That a monk should be a wizard—"

"A heretic, you mean!" The Bishop spoke with such vehemence that Heinrich was forced to admit he had indeed meant to say that. "He was no Christian at all, for though he professed devotion to the Son and the Holy Ghost, he heaped blasphemous scorn upon God the Father."

Questions of precedence among their three gods were a sore point with these carping clerics, and surely the last thing you wanted to get a bishop nattering about. An ill-considered word might provoke excommunication, which prevented your own wife from lying with you, or interrogation, which could prevent you from lying with anyone else's.

"Hugo's mother," the bishop went on, "was a foreigner and notorious spell caster, who boasted that she was the last of an ancient race of werefoxes who worshiped the demon Bacchus. My predecessor broiled those vapors out of her, you can be sure. Hugo himself is—was, I mean, thank you, dear graf!—obsessed with seeking the ancient clepsydra that, he said, the Father had set in motion to create Time itself. Hugo believed that by reversing this clock with hydromantic arts he could restore to mankind the eternal pleasures of Eden."

This sounded like some kind of wizard to Heinrich, but he nodded and tried to look orthodox. He apparently succeeded, for the bishop beamed at him and cried, "I think I'll grant you a plenary indulgence, you splendid blond beast, good for the rest of your life. In nomine, et cetera." The boy sketched a languid loop in the steam. "That covers every sin . . . except disobeying bishops."

Those who dared to irk Heinrich were routinely rebuked with five pounds of iron in the face. Even if he hadn't left his spiky gauntlet outside, he couldn't correct a bishop that way, at least not in the depths of a stronghold swarming with nominal clergymen who bore arms and were rumored to howl at the moon. It was clear that the bishop had farted, however, making the atmosphere even more intolerable. The graf set his hard face to granite lest it should show his disgust with the flatulent stripling.

"What do you want?" the bishop demanded of someone on Heinrich's blind side. He said to the graf: "That creature isn't with you, is it?"

Heinrich's left eye had been treacherously gouged out in his childhood by a Wend he had been strangling. He usually kept Reinhardt at his left hand to make up for this loss. Soft-hearted or not, Reinhardt could make a viper seem indecisive when his lord was threatened. But the invitation to the bath had not included his bodyguards. He swiveled his head to behold the drenched and dripping figure of Holy Hugo in the steam. This apparition, and not the bishop, exuded the feculent stench. Whatever relief this gave was canceled by the sight of the hermit's gray skin and milky eyes. With his jaw hanging slack and drooling river-bottom slime, he was plainly dead.

"Wotan!" Heinrich cried.

"Really, dear fellow, if there's one thing I can't abide, it's a persistence in superstitious, pagan—"

The revenant seized the bishop by the throat and lifted him, kicking and flailing, from his seat. Heinrich sprang upright. He was appalled to find himself cringing into a corner. He had never in his life reacted to a threat in that way, nor had he ever thought twice about dealing a blow. The extra moment gave his blow the force of a hammer but it was like striking a pond with a hammer. Fist and arm slipped through Hugo's liquid form, and Heinrich sprawled on the planks of the floor. At the same time he was drenched in a shockingly cold flood.

He was on his feet at once, but it was impossible to sort out his impressions of the last few seconds. He was soaked and shivering in the steam, as if someone had dumped a bucket of cold water over him, and he expected to confront the man who had done it. But no one stood before him. Holy Hugo was gone. The bishop lay contorted on the floor with a great purple plum stuffed in his gaping mouth: his tongue, Heinrich knew at once, the tongue of a strangled corpse. Blood oozed around the imprint of fingers in his fat neck.

"What?" someone demanded at his elbow. "What have you—?"

Unluckily for the skinny priest who quizzed him, Heinrich was again able to think. The occupants of this hellish stew had sensed only a violent disturbance in the steam. They had seen nothing. The graf slammed his fist down on the priest's tonsure and drove him to his knees.

"That will teach you not to kill bishops, foul heretic!"

No one of the soft, moist throng who pressed unpleasantly around Heinrich could contest this version of events. The priest he had struck couldn't. (This culprit's refusal to regain consciousness for a full week, despite unstinting application of hot irons, icy immersions and caustic enemas, proved that he was an obstinate sinner, and so the bishop's angry staff dropped his comatose body headfirst from the topmost spire of the cathedral. Except perhaps in a religious sense, this, too, failed to wake him).

Even as he elaborated on his tale of treason and heresy, the graf stared at the floor beneath his feet, where a quantity of water lay spilled. It rapidly seeped through the seams of the floorboards. No one else seemed to notice that it left behind some river weeds and a few twitching minnows and crayfish.

Heinrich bent to pick up a glimmering, pea-sized object that caught his eye among this wrack, but it skittered away from his fingers as if by design before dropping through the boards.

◆   ◆   ◆

As it always did, Heinrich's mood mellowed with the coming of long rains and long nights. In the twelve-foot bed that he shared with his principal heroes and their lemans, along with his favorite hounds and Wolfgang's beloved goat, it was sweet to sleep with the rain pattering and s plashing and gurgling all around; and sweet to couple, too, even though in his half-wakefulness he was sometimes uncertain whom or what he coupled with. By Christmas, when the glowworm-sun made only a perfunctory appearance that was often obscured by snow, he would be positively mewy. Heinrich was a creature of night and fog.

The resurrection of Holy Hugo no longer troubled him. He had known a shaman of the Wends who could raise the dead, he had known a rabbi of the Jews who could draw an image of a man in sand and have it rise up and walk, both to the extreme discomfiture of his simple-hearted Saxon warriors. That a wizard might remake himself from the water wherein he had drowned seemed commonplace.

Life is hard enough for the living, Heinrich knew, and a dead man labors under a further handicap. He bought a few masses for the repose of Holy Hugo's soul, hoping to increase his difficulties, for a vengeful spirit would surely be encumbered by a swarm of angels or demons striving to escort him to his eternal reward. The matter seemed closed.

These self-satisfied thoughts had crossed his mind when he drifted off on a night of particularly torrential rain. He was woken before dawn by a woman's piercing shrieks of outrage, disgust and, ultimately, puzzlement: "Help! Rape! I'm being . . . douched?"

The bed disgorged its inmates in a commotion of shouts and screams and barks. Candles were lit from the dying hearth, torches ignited. Swords were drawn to no purpose. Sleepy attendants and quidnuncs tumbled into the room to swell the uproar.

A lady called Sieglinde had caused the disturbance. Drenched and shivering, not just from cold but loathing, she babbled an incoherent account of her violation. She was closely attended, less for the nonsense she spoke than for her heedless display of wet charms. Brother Matthias, who bustled in to cover her with a blanket, was thwarted by a deft kidney-punch.

She asserted that a smelly intruder had raped her. In response to her violent struggles, he had not just doused her and half-drowned her but intimately injected her with icy water. All were prepared to dismiss this as a dream provoked by a fresh leak in the roof until it was remarked that three men had not yet stirred from the soaked bed, including Sieglinde's husband, Lothar. They had been strangled. A heavy silence fell, to be broken by Wolfgang's roar of grief upon discovering that his goat had suffered the same fate.

It was thought suspicious—especially by Brother Matthias, who further suspected the graf of nearly killing him with that cowardly blow—that Heinrich paid no further heed to the gleaming and goose-pimply Sieglinde, nor to the corpses on the bed, but turned from the scene to push aside the oiled linen that covered an embrasure and contemplate the continuing downpour: as if he found the weather more interesting than the outrages against his vassals.

◆　　◆　　◆

It took a week for the bed to dry, and Heinrich and his intimates were forced to sleep on the floor like ordinary people. This was especially galling to the hounds, who spent the livelong night pacing with clicking claws to find a comfortable spot, then twisting to screw themselves into its invisible limits, only to rise after fretful naps and pace again. Instead of throwing things at the dogs—and he was the only one who would have dared to—Heinrich observed them. On the night of the horrors, he had glimpsed Schrecklichen pursuing something that might have been a mouse, though it looked more like a bead of quicksilver, until she collided painfully with the wall. She had persisted in snuffling and growling and clawing at a seam in the stone blocks that appeared too narrow even for a mouse to squeeze through. On their rounds of the room, Schrecklichen and the other hounds now would give this chink a routine sniffing. Heinrich believed it was not just the absence of a bed that made them restless.

Although the graf was given to mad rages even when sober, and therefore seemed the obvious culprit, suspicion turned on Sieglinde as her story grew stranger with each retelling. Her marriage to Lothar had been tempestuous. Whenever he tried to beat her, she had bitten off one of his fingers, knocked out some of his teeth or stabbed him. He had shown off his domestic scars with greater pride than those he had earned in battle. "Who else dares to couple with a she-wolf?" he would demand as he flaunted his latest mutilation, and no one had the heart to answer: Just about everybody.

Once her guilt was established by consensus, a clamor arose to throw Sieglinde off the battlements, but Heinrich ordered that she instead take her vows at the convent of St. Horrida. Some grumbled that this was no punishment at all, exile to a bucolic spa where ladies whose liberty was deemed inconvenient wallowed in sapphism and vindictive prayer. But this debate was forgotten in outrage over a fresh enormity,

In his rounds of the countryside, Brother Matthias carried a flask for sprinkling holy water on infants, the sick and the occasional werewolf. Now that its silver finish had rubbed off, it seemed nothing more than a plain zinc flask; but Cardinal della Malebolgia, from whom the friar had bought it in Rome, had attested that this was the vessel Mary Magdalene had used to bring oil to the feet of Jesus. When it was stolen, its theft was seen as not just an inconvenience to Brother Matthias, not just an affront to Holy Mother Church, but as an assault against the majesty of God Almighty,

So Brother Matthias saw it, and his sermons scaled heights of fervor from which the Apocalypse might be viewed as a sunlit garden of moderation. His auditors did not merely hear about the tortures of the damned, they felt them as their flesh blistered from the heat and bled from the pricking of imps' tridents. The innocent threw fits and the wicked dropped dead before the torrent of fire that poured from his golden throat.

Satan, it was evident to everyone, had chosen to walk abroad in the domain of Heinrich von der Hiedlerheim. Although some ascribed this to the graf's murder of a holy man, not even Brother Matthias was so simple as to suggest it aloud.

But Satan himself was persuaded to stay at home by the cold that clamped down on the final month of the Year of Our Lord 980. The Millennium was not due for twenty years yet, but some scholars spent sleepless nights in a meticulous collation of Scriptures and the calendar, for the weather that now prevailed could portend nothing less than the end of the world.

In Ostenburg, it was said, fires froze on the hearths. When a peasant who had set out to bring a sample of this wonder to his lord stopped for refreshment in a warm tavern, the fire thawed inside his smock and burned him to ashes. Searchers who retrieved the frozen body of a woodcutter in the vicinity of Dimnitz happened to drop the corpse, which broke into innumerable tiny crystals that were seized and scattered by the wind.

With the cold came snow in every conceivable variety and permutation, in feathery flakes and wet wads, in stone bullets and steely darts, sometimes lit by unseasonable lightning in godless shades of pink and green. Strong men groveled before not only the fury but also the whimsicality of their Maker.

As he had known it would, Heinrich's mood lightened in the cold and darkness: so much so that those who already believed he was possessed were persuaded that a new and infinitely worse demon had set up residence. After a night and a day and most of another night of relentless drinking, he mounted naked to battlements slicked with black ice and, shaking his fist at a gale of granular snow, raved at its inability to harm him.

He was lifted like a cowslip and hurled downward by an unexpected gust, but the snow was so deep at the foot of the ramparts that he rose laughing and hurled snowballs at his would-be rescuers.

♦   ♦   ♦

Under the influence of his wife, Hrotswilda, a fastidious lady of the Franks, Heinrich strove to set an example of gentility for his household. At the riotous feast on Christmas Eve, when he felt an urgent need to relieve his bladder, he made a point of stepping outside to the courtyard.

Others, he reflected as he lifted his tunic, might have minded the icy gravel that ground his face, the importunate cold that instantly froze the mucus in his drooping mustache, but to him these proved that Holy Hugo was powerless. The ghost had incarnated himself from the water of a river, from a deluge of rain, but how could he fashion a useful body from stiff ice? Heinrich guffawed as his hot stream pierced the snow.

He had drunk deeply. Minutes passed as he hummed a tune, impressed his personal mark on the snow, stared up at the battering sleet, looked down to watch the steam rise . . .

An instant before it happened, he knew that he had grossly tempted fate. He had challenged Hugo, who now rose before him as a yellow mist. He tried to stop, knowing that increased micturition only gave strength to the revenant, but he might as well have tried to stem the torrent of the Edelwesel by his will alone. Spraying urine that further solidified the apparition, he groped for the sword that he had left behind him in the great hall. Slimy hands gripped his throat.

"Begone to hell, clock-seeking, Father-mocking son of a witching bassarid!" he cried, but those few who misheard their lord over the uproar of the feast assumed that he had barked his shin and was venting his fury in characteristic style.

Hard blows were not new to Heinrich, and he knew how they tended to baffle. But to ignore that initial bafflement, to resist the temptation to explore the question, "What has happened to me?": that way lay victory.

He punched, he kicked, he bit, and the answer gradually came to him that he had been flung back on the ice of the courtyard, taking a fearful knock to his skull and spine. He spat in the yellow face of the demon, which only drew strength from the liquid addition.

If a human foe had tried this absurd method of attack, Heinrich would simply have gripped his assailant's wrists and torn them away, or burst them outward with his own strong wrists, but this could not be done. His hands fumbled vainly in the mist of the phantom forearms while the grip on his neck stayed hard as iron. The thing's body was likewise insubstantial. He might as well have tried to bite fog or knee a moonbeam in the crotch.

It seemed to the graf that his brain had so swelled that it might erupt through his ears and eyeballs. That agony faded as a calm crept into his soul. The demon's face seemed far away, perceived down the length of a dark tunnel, and what did the struggle matter? Heinrich knew this tranquil phase for what it was, and the last, dim scrap of his spirit roused itself to die fighting. Still groping by reflex for his absent sword, his hand closed on the zinc flask he had stolen and kept by him all these weeks. What had he meant to do with it? He hardly knew, but he pulled the stopper and jammed the mouth between his attacker's eyes.

The grip vanished, and the ghost with it. He was drenched by a sudden flood, then hammered with freezing sleet. Coughing, retching, he braced his torso up on one trembling elbow before spewing his Christmas dinner. Through all this he kept the flask firmly plugged, although the captive soul rattled and raged and pricked his thumb cruelly. With infinite care, he replaced his thumb with the stopper and drove it home tight.

No man living, and few dead or unborn, could match the high deeds of Heinrich von der Hiedlerheim. But now he had triumphed in the most desperate struggle of his life; and all that anyone ever said about it—most pointedly Hrotswilda, with cruel allusion to swinish debauchery and premature senility—was that he had made a stinking mess of himself.

THE UNKNOWN ELIXIR
Dan Clore

Take a Coëtanean dog and an Armenian bitch. Join them together, and those two will beget for you a male puppy of celestial hue: and that puppy will guard you in your house from the beginning, in this World and the Other. What the hell was that supposed to mean? Elssinore had discovered many cryptic statements in the Bibliotheque de l'Abbaye de Saint-Crapauld, but the words of Hali, Philosopher and King of Arabia, as set forth in his Secret, tended to exceed the others in the obscurity of the symbolism of their Qabalahistic ciphers. He felt exceedingly inclined to put the volume in with those which he had finished studying, but that grouping now included all save the one he now held in his hand, which he had set aside more than once, to read later on, when he should have the background knowledge required to sound its mysteries more fully. But at this point, he realized that nothing lay in the study of the subject of the philosopher's stone but futility.

It did not correspond to the truth, then:—the rumor which had circulated through the village of Ximes for a century, that whoever had the daring to explore the secret recesses of the library of the ruinous Abbaye de

Saint-Crapauld should find out the mystery. But after reading every tome that resided in that monastery, he had not discovered that, the dream of which, had excited his brain from the earliest days of his life. Must he then give up, a failure?

As these thoughts traversed the corridors of his consciousness, he heard a rumbling sound as of an enormous belching. Again, the eructation re-echoed. And again, for a third time. It seemed to have come from directly beneath him. But nothing, he knew, lay beneath that chamber, at the bottom of the abbey. He crouched, and began to dig at the edges of the flagstone beneath him, which soon came loose. Once some seven or eight flags had been removed, a great hole gaped in the floor. He gazed down, holding his lantern to see into that sunless abyss, deeper than the well of Democritus (as his scholar's mind put it), and he discerned within the dark recesses the formless bulk of a couchant mass. The mass stirred a little, and put forth a huge and toad-shaped head. A nauseating foetor rose up to greet him. The abomination's eyelids fluttered as it glanced up with lambent coals inside two narrow slits, and then it spread seraphic wings and slowly arose, not moving its wings. A nimble and iridescent aureole surrounded the warts and wrinkles of its greenish and glistening skin.

The obvious realization occurred to the young man: this creature, whatever its nature, must know the secret. He inquired of it whether that were the case or no.

The thing, pot-bellied and crouching in the posture of a statue of the Buddha, replied that, from its appearance, one might better judge it an anti-Midas than an alchemist; that changing gold into lead might better match its talents than the converse; and that it might, through its mere touch and not through any expertise in the spagyric arts, mutate the known universe into a shapeless dungheap relieved only by rivulets of bilious slime and oceans of foetid ochre. It clutched its écru underbelly, turned a little bit to its left, and launched a jet of acrid vomit, filled with still-living slugs, worms, and woodlice which soiled the several piles of books that lay scattered thereabouts as they crept away in a daze.

But the youth knew the sort of ruse to expect from such a one. For all of the authorities avow that the philosopher's stone (which some, in their ignorance, have foolishly mislabeled the sorcerer's stone), the elixir, does not make vulgar gold, but rather, what they picturesquely termed philosopher's gold. This constitutes not a means to gain gaudy trinkets, unworthy of a superior mind, not wholly confined to the material, but rather, it confers enlightenment and immortality upon the one who drinks it, finely powdered and mixed with liquor. Furthermore, an unsightly appearance could not rule out the being's knowledge: for do not the Holy Scriptures describe the Omnipotent in even more fearsome, if not outright uncanny and eldritch, terms? And do not the more redoubtable Elder Ones exceed even that depiction, in terms both of dreadfulness and arcane knowledge?

Yes, but how did the youth know that he did not find himself face to face with a demon?

And if he did? Does not the word *demon* reflect its proper etymology and meaning, from the Greek *daimon* or *daemon*, such as the universally admired Daimon of Socrates, as set forth by Apuleius, in his work of that title? And does not this in turn correspond with the Augoeides of Pythagoras, (consult his Life, by Iamblichus, perhaps in a less-bestained copy than the one over there), and the Holy Guardian Angel of Abramelin, portrayed in the book of his Sacred Magick, given by Abraham the Jew unto his son Lamech? Which demonstrates well enough its inability to tell its client a falsehood, does it not?—

The entity conceded in the argument, and admitted that it had the much sought-after récipé. But it could only reveal it on a certain condition. The recipient must know that: while, truly enough, his brain would never cease functioning, nor his heart pumping blood, the elixir carries, as well—a terrible burden. For the youth, once he had partaken of it, would "become as a sign unto the generations of men, of what human life means, and what it can become, if it were only to reach its ultimate fulfillment."

The youth readily consented, finding the latter condition not at all unwelcome. He could hardly do any less, after all, for his fellows. The thing described the process, which for good reason we will not detail in this place—not wishing to compromise the reader—and departed on motionless wings, leaving a trail of unctuous and ebullient slime in its wake.

♦   ♦   ♦

The deserted abbey became a series of laboratories for the next nine months. Flashes of lightning illuminated the building's ruins, and innumerable alembics and retorts filled the rooms where monks had formerly slept. Finally, the pregnant pot gave forth with the stone, and the young man's project had succeeded. He ground the stone, which had the size and shape of the ball of dung impelled by the radiant scarab-beetle, not a well-known species in those latitudes, in a mortar. He mixed the powder with a bottle of red wine, which he had purchased in Ximes, at the onset of his researches, sparing no expense, so as to celebrate his victory at the same time as he should consummate it. He swallowed the bottle in a single draught.

There appeared to Elssinore's vision the creature which had previously given him the récipé, as it alighted from a flight on its hesitant wings; and as he felt the potion take effect, his vision blurred, and when he cleared his eyes, instead of the unknown monstrosity he beheld waves of greyed hair and the billows of a wrinkled forehead. The identity of the human before him had been plainly revealed to his consciousness by the defaced features of the man's defeatured face. For, while traveling from the Faroe Islands on their way to France, he and his parents had stopped over in England, and there they had heard the frightful Legend of Lord Weÿrdgliffe, who from his earliest years had never laughed like others did. The Legend continued, whispered by the lips of persons over-given to the reading of Gothick Romances and Shilling Shockers, that one day he had finally resolved to do it, and that he left off writing his objectionable Tales of Terror, and as he as he stood before a mirror in the mansion-house on his ancestral estates, the Waughters, he took a penknife with a steel edge, and split the flesh at the places where the lips meet. After a few minutes of comparison, after he had cleared the blood that flowed abundantly from the twin wounds, he saw full well that this wasn't the laughter of others!— But a strange pride consumed him, and he denied that this meant that he wasn't laughing, and claimed, that, in fact, only he truly knew how to laugh, and he resolved that he had in fact succeeded—only too well—and that others would see the point of the jest that could produce such a grimace, even if he would have to topple the entire universe, overthrow God, Satan, and the more dreadful Outside Things, to make them do it—(Having succeeded in something as difficult as laughing, he didn't acknowledge any limits to his powers)—At this unwelcome recognition, Elssinore began to fear that he had only prepared himself to become the butt of some incomprehensible practical joke—

The master of Unwarranted Metamorphoses spoke: "I believe that you have somewhat misjudged the character of my words, which in some cases carry a certain burden of ambiguity, which can have a dolorous significance for their misinterpreter." He seized an anvil—at first he wanted to use a hammer, but decided that such a light instrument would not produce the desired effect—and hurled it at the forehead of the unfortunate, who fell insensate beneath the blow. Lord Weÿrdgliffe knew well enough that the effect would not outlast the moment, and he immediately stripped the young man of clothing and sliced off his eyelids with a penknife. Then he took up a razor-sharp axe, and whacked off the youth's arms, legs, and genitalia, which he threw to a pair of hedgehogs, who didn't turn down that generous offer. From each of the novel apertures formulated by that mutilation, blood spurted as though from bottomless and unfathomable fountains. The Baron grabbed the beautiful youth by his hair of gold and carried him to the top of the highest tower in the ruinous abbey. He swung him around like a sling, soaking the abbey's surroundings in gushing jets of blood, until, at a precisely calculated moment, correlated with the swiftness of movement to create a certain well-specified angle, he instantly arrested the motion of his arm of ironical iron, which had as its effect: the youth's hair ripped lose from his head, sending the torso—launched by the centrifugal force—flying towards the stars (he did not smash into an oak-tree), and leaving the Baron with a beautiful, blond mane in his hand.

They say that, when Lord Weÿrdgliffe runs through the fields, steeped in some fit of mental alienation and lunacy, as though surfeited with an incommensurable pride by the ultimate fulfillment of his anterior designs mingled with the poignant pangs of an implacable conscience, chased by the little children and old women, who throw rocks at him, as if he were a blackbird, clutching a blood-soaked mane in his hand, holding it to his breast, nobody connects it with the eldritch, crimson comet, which, according to the credulous beliefs of superstitious peasants, priests, and kings, returns periodically (even though no one has yet determined the exact law governing its occulted orbit) to the earth, to appear in the heavens, dripping a drizzling scarlet rain of misty blood onto the farms, castles, churches, and everything, and foretelling disaster and calamity to come for all who behold it. Even the peasants disbelieve the testimony of the most keen-sighted among seers, who aver that once they had wiped their far-focused lenses of the ruddy liquid which had besmeared them, they would behold, concentrating their gaze upon the spot in the sky where the heavenly body should have appeared, a limbless trunk, attached to a hairless head. The most far-seeing of them all froze in terror, muttering only, "*Jambebleu!— Jarnicotondieu!*—That expression—on its face—horror—" No further revelations were forthcoming from the astounded gazer, who immediately entered a monastery and took an irretractable vow of eternal silence. They say that those few of good conscience wish that an enormous black cloud would swallow up the sun, the moon, the stars, and the will-o'-the-wisps of the swampy morasses—If only its omnipotent darkness might efface the unwelcome awareness brought on by the sanguinary meteor.

—Lord Weÿrdgliffe, the Waughters

RILE FOUTS AND DEAD JAKE SORREL

Lawrence Barker

RILE FOUTS REMOVED HIS BROAD-BRIMMED HAT—the one that saw him through one hail of Billy Yank's Minié balls at Lookout Mountain and another at Chicamauga—and studied the sky. The setting sun peeked through dark threatening clouds, hanging over the Smokies like the angry breath of Jehovah might have looked had the Final Trump blown back in the February of Bitter '67.

Rile pulled his last plug of Carolina tobacco—the herb of the green hills closest to God's heart—out of his pouch. It rested, hard and black as the soul of a plat-eye, the worst booger to tramp the Tennessee mountains, in his hand.

"Don't you know nothing?" the baritone voice of Sinner Man, the red-eyed mule that carried his rifle, provisions, and, most importantly, his fiddle, bellowed. "How you going to shoe away Old Horny-foot if you chew up your Carolina?"

Rile leaned against a moss-covered chestnut stump, the dark plug of tobacco in his hand. "Everybody knows tobacco's the blessed herb.

One whiff of its smoke—even that jim-tar weed from down Macon way—makes most Devil's handymen rabbit like Kentucky volunteers getting their first taste of grape-shot."

Sinner Man's tail swung back and forth, as though batting invisible flies. "Old Horny-foot ain't *most*. He's more bull-of-the-woods than handyman. Don't plan on nothing short of the best sending him high-tailing, and maybe not that."

Rile turned the tobacco over and over, considering it like a Charleston jeweler contemplates a shiny diamond ring.

"You ain't going to save it, are you?" the mule sighed, as if he knew the answer already.

Rile idly uprooted a jewel-weed and wrapped it about his wrist. "A chew sure would soften the miles," he said, his gravelly voice a sharp contrast to the mule's sonorous tones. "Besides, tobacco ain't the only way of sending your old master skedaddling."

Sinner Man tossed his head as though a deer-fly the size of a Carpetbagger's avarice had hold of his ear. "How long you think your luck will last?"

Rile shrugged. He bit the plug in half. The tobacco lay, serpent-kiss bitter, on his tongue, and then with a sigh Rile slipped the rest back into his pouch. With deep satisfaction, he began chewing.

Rile's eyes danced. He let the jewel-weed drop, and raising his hands to playing position, pantomimed fingering the notes of *Old Bangham*.

"I've out-fiddled Old Horny-foot every last time."

Sinner Man's jaws snapped a tender young leaf off a sassafras bush. "Dang fool," the mule snorted, chewing on the leaf. "You lose once and you're his. Won't never escape."

Rile turned his head and spat a great brown mass of ambeer into the tangle of Virginia Creepers dangling from the trees. "I notice you managed."

"And you also notice," Sinner Man said, his great red eyes surveying his hulking form, "Old Horny-foot made a few alterations in me and cursed me to follow you because I danced to your fiddling like nobody never did to his." Sinner Man stamped his feet, as though attempting a Virginia Reel.

Rile's brow furrowed. An image of Sinner Man, in the no-creature-of-God's-green-Earth form he had worn before Old Horny-foot changed him, danced in his memory. "You ain't saying you miss looking how you used to, are you?"

"I'm just saying that maybe it would have been better if, instead of fiddling, you'd have sung," Sinner Man continued, making the last word go as off-key as Rile's attempts at vocalizing. "Then we'd both be pulling Old Horny-foot's wagon."

Rile laughed and stuck out his hand. A raindrop, cold and piercing, struck his palm and ran down the wrist. "At least we'd be under some sort of barn-shed. I can't say I relish sleeping in the elements." Rile rubbed his back, counting the nights since he and Sinner Man had last slept under a roof. "Make yourself useful, and tell me if there's a settlement in these parts. Ain't many that won't trade a night's barn-shelter for an hour's fiddle-sawing."

Sinner Man raised his great head and sniffed. "Over that rise," the mule said, flinging his head in the direction of the next ridge, "there's a pine-wood fire and somebody cooking polk-stalks and kale. Half hour's walk, more if the way's steep."

"I reckon that's where we're going."

Sinner Man snorted and backed up, prancing like an ordinary mule does when it smells a bear. "Greens ain't all that's there, Rile."

Rile frowned. "What else?"

"Don't rightly know. Something that sends spider-legs over my back." Sinner Man's tail twitched nervously. "Maybe we should keep walking. One more night's rain won't hurt none."

Rile squinted at the ridge. It seemed darker and more bramble-grown than it had a few minutes ago. "Maybe not," he whispered.

As if in response, a jagged lightning streak painted the sky bone white. "No sir," Rile said, shaking his head. "I don't care for storms." Faraway thunder rolled. "Too much like the Yankee cannon at Moses' Creek." He rose up, walking toward the ridge. "You coming?"

A distant mountain cat screamed. Two long, sharp cries, and then it fell silent.

"No common sense," Sinner Man snorted. "Save me from fools and fiddlers." Placing one foot after the other, he followed Rile up the ridge.

•   •   •

The cabin, weather-worn and gray, stood on a creek-stone foundation. To one side sat a little smoke-house, to the other a lean-to. From the cabin's river-rock chimney rose a finger of shadowy smoke, coiling and turning like a French Broad River copperhead.

Rile tucked his ancient fiddle underneath his arm. "Hello the house," he called, the universal warning of approach.

A shutter rattled, as though some invisible watcher peered out.

"Something ain't right," Sinner Man mumbled, shaking his head as he ambled into the lean-to.

"Hush," Rile said. The door creaked open a hand's breadth. "Some folks don't cotton to uppity animals."

A woman, chestnut hair pulled back in a bun, peered out, hands locked about the door like a lost soul clinging to Hell's gates. "Get gone, stranger." Sad old eyes peered out of her smooth young face. "Ain't no fitting place."

"Ma'am," Rile said, doffing his hat, "I'm just a poor wanderer, hoping for shelter." Rile stepped onto the porch, boards creaking beneath his weight.

The woman silently mouthed alarm-words. "Go away," they might have been.

Sinner Man snorted, as if to say, "I told you so." Rile looked back and shook his head. No overwrought mule was about to make him spend another night in the woods.

Rile bowed his head. "I would sure appreciate the use of your porch, or lean-to, or whatever quarters you see fit to share."

"Edom, we got company?" a voice, croaking like a strangled turkey buzzard, echoed from within the cabin. The woman cringed and glanced back into the darkness. "Don't idle like an Ohio drummer," the voice continued, "Invite the man in."

The woman's eyes fell. "We'd be pleased to have you sit a spell, stranger." Her fingers tugged at her worn gingham dress, wrinkling its ragged cloth.

Rile stuck out his hand. "Ain't no stranger. I'm Rile Fouts."

The woman limply brushed her hand against his finger. "I'm Edom Sorrel," she said, opening the door a bit.

A stone fireplace dominated the cabin's far end, a kale-filled, black iron pot steaming above the fire. From the ceiling hung dried herbs and brick red peppers. A brown and gray striped woven rug sheltered the puncheon floor, two ladder-back chairs and a spinning wheel atop it. Skin-wool rags blanketed the windows.

Edom swung the door completely open. A figure, tin plate in hand, sat on an unfinished bench beside the fire. A gray uniform's tattered remnants hung from its spare frame.

The figure stood and turned.

Boiled-egg eyes, deep sunk in waxy gray skin, stared out at Rile. A web of black veins traced a path over pustuled arms, white bone gleaming through. Firelight shone though the gap, Yankee cannon ball sized and shaped, in the man's gray-flesh belly.

Rile tugged at his collar. Distant thunder rumbled.

Well, it wasn't like Rile had never met the rambling dead before.

Weren't all of them bad, either.

The man lifted a fork of kale to his mouth and carefully chewed. He swallowed. A moment later, the kale fell through the hole in his middle and sloshed to the floor.

146

"This," Edom said, gesturing at the figure, "is my husband, Jake. Dead Jake Sorrel, they call him in these parts."

◆　　　◆　　　◆

Rile sat in a ladder-back chair, silence pressing down like a weighted shroud as Dead Jake Sorrel chewed one mouthful after another. Rile glanced at Edom. The woman's eyes stayed fixed on the flax on her wheel, as though the rest of the cabin were only a cold-potato-and-gravy bad dream.

Rile sadly shook his head. Wasn't the first time he had seen a young widow bury herself when her man wouldn't admit to dying. Every case seemed sadder than the last, though.

"Good to see a new face," Dead Jake croaked, finishing his kale. "Don't many folks come around here no more."

"Don't imagine so," Rile replied. Edom's spinning slowed, her lips trembling. Rile, pretending not to notice, threw another pine chunk on the fire.

"Used to go to Townsend," Dead Jake continued, nodding in the direction of the village a half-day's walk down the valley, "to howdy folks, to dance in Old Man Noah King's barn, to swap farm goods for amenities." He shook his head, a trail of black fluid oozing down his slack jaw. "Folks just turned against us, though."

Edom sighed. The flax between her fingers came to a halt.

"I can see it might get a tad lonely," Rile said. "Besides company, what's in Townsend? Didn't look like much when I passed through."

Dead Jake shrugged. His bones grated like a bear trap. "Whiskey. Yankees took the copper tubing. Ain't nobody what will sell us no more," Jake added in explanation.

Rile raised his eyebrow. "Begging your pardon, but a lot of ladies don't take to their men using corn squeezings," he said, nodding in Edom's direction.

"I might have minded once," Edom replied, voice hollow as a Sharpsburg hogshead. "Not no more though."

"Pretty fabric for the woman," Jake continued, ignoring his wife. Edom shifted uncomfortably, as though not caring to be reminded of her weary dress.

"And tobacco," Jake croaked. "Last spring's rains up and drowned out our crop. Ain't had a plug since."

Edom's fingers pulled at the flax.

Rile leaned back in his chair and stared into the dancing red flames. The sound of his breathing rasped heavily in his ears.

"What I wouldn't give," Edom cried, voice cracking, "for a good chew."

"You're going to have to learn to go without," Dead Jake snapped. He drummed his fingers on the bench, every tap leaving a black mark. "We both have to learn to go without things we enjoy." He lifted his feet and rotated his ankles, dry bones creaking like a black tupelo after the first frost. "You got any idea how long it's been since these old hooves dusted Noah King's barn to the tune of *Billy Grimes* or *Old Judge Duffy*?"

Rile watched the dancing flames for several minutes. Rising, he stamped his foot. "Yankee greed might rule the land," he said, bowing to Edom, "but chivalry is not dead." With a flourish, be reached into his pouch and drew out his Carolina.

"For you, ma'am."

"You sure?" Her eyes darted nervously.

"Positive." Rile forced the plug into her hand.

"He's done and done it," Edom called, leaping from her chair and clutching the tobacco to her breast. "You can take him now."

A bulge, like a great leech rising from lowland mud, formed in the rug. With a bass rumbling, it shaped itself into the gray and brown mottled form of Old Horny-foot, a wicked and hungry look on his hatchet-shaped face. With his four jointed talons, Old Horny-foot tipped his kepi and withdrew his three-string, teardrop-shaped black fiddle from his back-pouch.

"You surrendered your protection," he sneered, blowing his hog-fat-and-lye breath in Rile's face. "That wasn't smart." He flexed his toes, so the antlers sprouting from between them rattled like musical bones.

Rile glanced at his hosts. Dead Jake sat as impassively as a Yankee officer ordering a town's burning. Edom cowered in the corner, terror in her eyes. Rile nodded to himself. So Edom and Jake were Old Horny-foot's, to use as that bark-skinned scoundrel saw fit. Well, lots of folks found themselves in that position these days.

Rile reached for his fiddle. "I beat you before. You know the rules."

"I most certainly do." Old Horny-foot stamped about the cabin, the floor shaking with his every move. "Now we will see who is the fiddle's master."

Rile raised his bow.

Old Horny-foot's steel grip closed about Rile's wrist. "This time," he said, a coal-oil grin on his lips, "I go first." Rile pulled away from Old Horny-foot's corpse-cold claw, nodded and put down his bow.

Old Horny-foot planted his fiddle against his chest. One at a time, he plucked the strings, adjusting the pitch of the third one up a hair.

"Get on with it," Rile snarled.

Old Horny-foot ran his bow across the strings, swirling and bending notes in the same style as the Irish fiddler that had saved a nearly-dead Rile from the bloody surgeons at Petersburg.

Rile felt a drop of sweat run down his side. Some folks say the Devil himself is an Irishman. To judge by how Old Horny-foot took to Gaelic fiddling, it just might be so.

Old Horny-foot patted his foot and began playing. He made the notes of *The Old Horned Sheep* ring like a babbling brook. Without warning, he switched to *The Rambling Pitchfork*, sending that brook echoing off bluffs of silver and gold and, to close, he switched tempos and played a heart-rending version of *Do You Want Anymore?*, ending on a note that made you think he was about to start over, but instead sat down his fiddle. "Would you like to capitulate, or must we sully ourselves with an unseemly struggle?"

Rile ran his bow across the strings. "I ain't giving up."

Old Horny-foot bowed, an oily smirk on his lips.

Rile searched hard, looking for something he could play better than what Old Horny-foot had just done. It couldn't be *House Carpenter* or *Lazarus*. Not even *Little Bessie*, his best foot-stomper. He'd used every one of them before.

Dead Jake's finger bones popped like shot from distant smooth-bores.

Well, Dead Jake liked *Billy Grimes*. That old tune would do.

Rile brought the bow to his fiddle and played as he never had before, bouncing the melody between the first and last two strings. He filled every break with double grace-notes, and every pause with long and short rolls. He made his fiddle sound like a gold-beaked she-dove, calling her long-lost lover.

Before he was half through the second verse, Dead Jake Sorrel leapt up. "Fiddling to gladden angels' aching hearts," he shouted. His feet began twitching, keeping time with the music.

Edom gasped, clutching the plug tightly.

Rile paid her no mind. He just fiddled until the last note of the fifth verse, and then stopped. As he did, Dead Jake froze.

"That was pretty good," Old Horny-foot grudgingly admitted. "Can you top this?"

Old Horny-foot tightened the tension of his bow. His fingers moved like lightning, calling the notes of *The Unfortunate Rake* from the black instrument, happy and sad at the same time. Before he reached the second repeat, he switched to *Farewell to My Troubles*, notes sounding like diamond raindrops on a gold-shingled roof. He ended with a double-time version of *The Gallowglass*, his extra finger joints letting him add notes no human fiddler could match.

Old Horny-foot sat down his fiddle. "One more thing," he said. "Don't you think it unfair that you have four strings and I only have three?" With an unctuous grin, Old Horny-foot's claw severed Rile's second string. "Your turn," Old Horny-foot beamed.

Rile's mind raced. Damn, Old Horny-foot was good. Maybe even better than Rile at his best.

A crash of thunder, sounding as though it came from Old Horny-foot's pouch, shook the cabin. "Does thunder make you nervous?" Old Horny-foot asked. "So sorry." His head shook in mock sympathy.

Rile's hands trembled. Sweat beaded on his brow.

And the worst part was that all he could think of was a tired old chestnut that all the fiddlers had long ago beaten to death, *Old Judge Duffy.*

If *Old Judge Duffy* it was, that was what it would be.

Rile started playing.

First straight, then adding long rolls and bowed triplets.

Good, but not good enough to cap Old Horny-foot.

If he only had another instrument off of which to play—a banjo or gut-bucket or even a voice, singing the words about the judge hanging the innocent washerman the town didn't need in place of the vital, but guilty blacksmith.

With a thunderous crash, the cabin's door collapsed. It was Sinner Man, rear hooves a battering ram. The mule turned and shoved his head through the door. Sinner Man's rich baritone picked up the words to *Old Judge Duffy.*

"Better than Noah King's," Dead Jake Sorrel croaked. He began a stiff-jointed clog-step.

Rile played harder and faster, braiding notes up and down, over and around Sinner Man's vocal framework. Never missing his broken string.

Dead Jake danced harder and, with a rifle-crack, his left arm broke off at the shoulder and tumbled to the floor. Dancing all the harder and jiggling to the music, his nose sloughed off, bouncing at his feet. In rapid succession, his lower jaw and a fist-sized chunk of chest-flesh followed.

"Enough foolishness," Old Horny-foot growled. "The competition has ended. You have lost." He reached for Rile.

"Don't stop playing," Edom shouted, a light shining in her eyes.

Rile jumped back, so Old Horny-foot's claw missed him by an arm's-length. Rile played harder and faster, weaving a countermelody above Sinner Man's deep rich singing.

Dead Jake danced harder.

With a mighty crack, Dead Jake Sorrel snapped at the middle. For a minute, his two halves hung together, like he didn't know he had broken.

Then his top collapsed into the fire, while his bottom crumbled to a heap of bones and dried flesh.

Edom whooped in triumph. "I might be your play-pretty," she shouted to Old Horny-foot, "but this here fiddler got shed of my husband. That's a dang sight better than *you* ever did." She raised Rile's Carolina over her head.

Old Horny-foot's eyes bulged like an unmilked cow's udders.

"Don't you dare," he shouted, pointing a long taloned finger at Edom as the realization of what she was about to do entered his head. "You do, and I'll see that you envy your rotting husband."

"Do your worst," Edom shouted. "I've already been through Hell." She kicked her husband's crumbling remains and turned to Rile. "Take it," she shouted, tossing the plug.

With a catamount howl, Old Horny-foot dove for Rile, claws raking the air.

Rile dropped his bow and, keeping his fiddle out of harm's way, dodged under Old Horny-foot's talons and caught the plug.

"The Injuns' conjure men taught them to send your kind hightailing," Rile shouted. "A Carolina Cherokee taught me."

With fluid grace, Rile rolled to the fire, Old Horny-foot just behind him. Rile lit the tobacco, raised the smoldering plug and blew the acrid fumes directly into Old Horny-foot's face.

Old Horny-foot screamed. The smoke, scalding him like boiling water, turned his flesh from mottled gray to bright pink. Old Horny-foot retreated, hands clamped over his face.

Rile felt weather-beaten fingers lock about his free hand. It was Edom. "Thank you," she whispered.

Old Horny-foot sputtered, the gray coming back into his face. "You've won a reprieve, fiddler," he growled, voice echoing like Yankee cannon. His claws raked the air. "The lady," he said, eyeing Edom, "chose to pay your toll. My house-servants will make sure she pays it long and hard."

On the porch, Sinner Man shuddered, as if he understood more than Rile could ever dream.

"Whatever comes, it was worth it," Edom replied, lower jaw jutting defiantly. Her hand slipped from Rile's.

"Wait a minute," Rile demanded.

"Don't think this is over," he rumbled, yellow eyes glowing with wild-hog rage.

Then, suddenly, Old Horny-foot, Edom, the cabin—everything—all sank like a blown-up bladder with the air being let out.

Rile found himself standing among the bare stones of an old tumble-down cabin's ruined foundation.

No sign of the confrontation with Old Horny-foot.

Except for Sinner Man, giving Rile a fish-eyed stare and disdainfully chewing a sassafras leaf.

Rile looked upward. Wind parted the clouds, letting pinpoint stars shine through. He picked up his bow and, striding over to the mule, deposited his fiddle, bow, and Carolina in Sinner Man's pack.

"I reckon we roost under the stars after all," Rile said, nodding slowly.

"Reckon so," Sinner Man replied. The mule sniffed the air. "This is as good a place as any. Smells clean, all newly washed."

Rile nodded, pulling his blankets from the mule's bags. "In the morning, we start early."

"Start early?"

"I got me a hankering to dangle my toes in the Mississippi," Rile answered, spreading the blankets beneath an overhanging hemlock tree. "It will take a mort of walking to get there." He lay down on the blanket.

Sinner Man cringed. "Old Horny-foot lives on the Mississippi," he mumbled.

"Reckon so," Rile replied.

"You ain't thinking of paying him a call, are you?"

"Are Old Horny-foot's house-servants likely to be at his lodgings?" Sinner Man nodded.

Rile yawned. "Then so is someone I owe a mighty big favor. Rile Fouts pays his debts."

Sinner Man sighed. "No common sense," the mule snorted, shaking his head. "Save me from fools and fiddlers." Folding his legs beneath him, he lay down beside Rile.

THE CHALLENGE FROM BELOW
Robert M. Price
Peter Cannon
Donald R. Burleson
Brian McNaughton

Part One: Under the Mound
by Robert M. Price

HE LOOKED AT THE ANCIENT CYLINDER and was not surprised. Not even at the unusual caste of the metal, which was an indefinable hue of blue-gray. There was nothing like verdigris or tarnish on it, though, for all he knew, those who had unearthed it might have scraped away such encrustation before delivering it to him. Without having to spend time puzzling over how the tube was meant to be opened, as he had many times with other artifacts, he found the catch piece at once and unscrewed the top. Sure enough, there was a rolled set of sheets inside. These he reclined to peruse. This is what he read:

I was saddened, not particularly surprised, at the news of the death of the ancient Indian shaman Gray Eagle. I had expected it, dreaded it, for some time, for the medicine man was both ancient and dear to me. My connection with him is perhaps not unknown to you, my reader, whoever you may be, since my books sold well a dozen or so years ago. In *Gray Eagle Speaks*, I had simply interviewed the old man, as I wished to preserve the

155

intriguing bits of myth and tall tales of the frontier days Gray Eagle had
to share. Here was a genuine treasure trove of Native American lore with
few parallels to anything previous ethnologists had been able to gather. In
Soaring with the Eagle, I had recounted, with initial reluctance, some of the
remarkable initiatory visions I had undertaken under the tutelage of the
wizened sage. Though popular response was gratifying enough to justify
a series of four more volumes on the same theme, the book destroyed any
academic standing I had enjoyed among my colleagues. Most dismissed it
as fiction. I cannot blame them. I knew the risk I was taking, but believed
that knowledge is gained to be shared. Not to publish my findings would
have seemed almost a betrayal of some Hippocratic oath that all research-
ers implicitly take. And I suppose that is why I am taking the trouble to
write this account, and not exactly under optimum conditions.

On receipt of the news of my old mentor's death, I arranged at once
to fly out to Oklahoma, even though I knew there would be no funeral, at
least none that a white man would be allowed to attend. Nonetheless, I had
duties to perform. Gray Eagle had told me that one day he would disappear into the wilderness to die among the spirits of his people. I assumed
this had at last happened, though my informants had not known, or at
least not said, whether his body had been recovered. In any case, the old
shaman had instructed me in no uncertain terms what I should do. I was
to undertake one last vision quest amid the silent and ageless buttes and
mesas in the merciless sunlight and the impassive searchlight of the moon.
And this I prepared to do. Few provisions were necessary, even by way of
maps, for I knew the Oklahoma wastes well from my previous meditative
sojourns there.

Once I had arrived in Oklahoma, I hired a car to make my way to the
small settlement of Binger, a hamlet which seemed never to have experienced the expansion common to the towns of the region during the great
days of the oil boom. Maybe it was better that way: its fate was to have
started as a hamlet and, from the looks of it, to finish as one, somehow de-
clining despite never having reached a higher point. No one there, though
open and friendly, seemed to have any information to share with me. The

Indians kept to themselves, even more than in the old days. At least I knew no corpse had been discovered. So I struck out into the desert, fully expecting to lay the old man to his final rest, though I did not relish discovering him in the state of decomposition he must by now have assumed. Unless, as I hoped, my informant had seen to the task.

I had thought I knew the full extent of the local terrain very well, having covered a great deal of it on foot and in the flight-visions into which Gray Eagle had initiated me. But now, looming above me, was the mute silhouette of an ancient Indian burial mound. I knew at once that it must be the place about which several local legends and rumors circulated, the haunted mound where a headless giant was sometimes observed standing guard, where Father Yig, the Rattler King, held court. With a shudder I got out of the car and approached it. What I felt was by no means fear, but a strange intuition of uncertainty. One never knows what to expect in a vision quest, else there would be no point in undertaking it. But I began to sense what awaited me was something fundamentally more important, more powerful, if that makes any sense, than the already singular mission on which I had thought to embark. Would there be something atop the mound to justify my forebodings? Perhaps the wasted body of my friend? There was but one way to find out.

The ascent was easy enough, despite the unusual height of the mound, since such climbs are common in the work of the field anthropologist. Hunches, too, are the stock in trade of my profession, and I soon found that I had been half right, anyway. There was indeed a supine body at the top. I cannot say that it rested in death, for its contorted posture announced that death had come at the end of a fierce struggle. What manner of wilderness predator had attacked the man I could not readily guess. The wounds had been horrific. There was no longer any head attached to the tattooed torso. After a few moments' careful scrutiny I concluded that the man had not been of Indian stock, nor had he been so hideously dismembered in the final struggle. Incredibly, the tissue at the end of the neck-stump looked for all the world like old scar tissue. This was a forensic puzzle like none I had ever encountered. How could the manifest death wounds on limbs and chest looked so much more recent?

I looked over the edge of the mound to where my car was parked below and considered how best to load the carcass onto the vehicle. In order to avoid damaging the remarkable specimen further, I should have to arrange a makeshift harness and hauling line, though with the materials in hand, I could not see how this might be accomplished. So I left the problem for later and calculated what to do next. My directions to the place had been given me by Gray Eagle some years before, so it could not have been this strange corpse to which he had meant to direct me. There must be something else. And to that I must now turn. Archaeology would have to wait.

It was finally the shifting of the evening shadows, as the sun relented and began to sink, that revealed the open shaft leading downward. By a trick of optical illusion, the opening had been hidden in plain sight up until now. I unclipped my flashlight from my belt and did not hesitate to rush in where angels might fear to tread.

Given the aridity of the area, it was no surprise that the uneven walls of the descending shaft were free of nitre. At first I imagined that I was making my way gingerly through a natural crevasse in age-old rock—until I came to my senses and realized the obvious: that burial mounds are artificial structures. I had noticed details that might imply human craftsmanship, but these I had subconsciously dismissed. Now I realized they must indeed denote the hand of a designer, unless they denoted something quite fantastic. Could this possibly be a natural structure which happened to look like the work of the ancient Mound Builder cultures? Or, the crazy inspiration occurred to me, might this stony heap have served as the prototype for all the other mounds? Was it, like Moses' Mount Horeb, a natural edifice revered as sacred space because of its singular structural regularity, or because of some great event that had taken place here so long ago that even ancient Indian lore retained no trace of it? I could be sure of nothing except that at this point, in this odd place, no possible explanation, no matter how far-fetched, could yet be ruled out.

Down and down I went, never finding the going particularly rough (again, possibly implying human artifice), until I began to perceive that my flashlight no longer cut so stark a swath through the surrounding darkness. Could my high-power batteries be failing already? No, for I immediately realized, switching off the light, that the darkness about me had itself lightened considerably. From whence could this misty vapor of radiance be emanating? Were there unseen fissures to the surface that functioned as ventilators? This could not be, however, as I noticed the light had a queer bluish tinge to it. It was not natural sunlight, then. As my eyes adjusted to the vague half-light, I found I could see the ceiling above me in closer detail. It seemed to be carpeted with a coat of luminescent fungus or moss. That added up to one mystery solved, but only by another. I knew of no such species. Not a professional botanist, I was nonetheless fairly certain that no such organism was known. This was a day of strange and unsettling discoveries, and this was by no means to be the last of them.

The colors of the illumination seemed to shift toward the purplish end of the spectrum and to brighten, the further down I went. My watch had stopped somewhere along the line, and I had unaccustomed difficulty in estimating how many hours had passed in my descent. My feet and back had commenced to ache, and this surprised me, implying I had spent a great deal more time here than I consciously marked. I began seeing great tree-trunk-like pillars, which, to my relief, did not actually block my progress. At first I thought I had found definitive evidence of human artifice— until I noticed that the structures seemed to have been formed by the slow growing together of stalagmite and stalactite over many centuries.

The pillars, as I could not help regarding them, did manage to limit my field of vision until, suddenly emerging from between two of them, I stopped in my tracks, gazing slack-jawed at an astonishing panorama before me. Only a few feet away, the shaft widened drastically into the surface of a vast inner cavern. Traveling any faster along the rocky tunnel, I should certainly have plunged out unwittingly to fall to my death below, like rushing water reaching the end of a drainage pipe and flinging itself with futile momentum in an arc to the surface below. As it was, I had to use the greatest care to negotiate a sliding path down the precipitous, nearly vertical, wall of rock slanting down and away from the tunnel-hole.

I was a moment gaining my bearings. First I made sure of my footing and, before descending, I scanned the scene before me. It was good that I had troubled to secure firm footing, since what I next beheld would have been sufficient to bowl me over. I now saw not merely a cavern outstretched below and beyond me, but a virtual world. The actual extent of it could not even be guessed, but it seemed to extend for ever and ever. The tunnel mouth from which I had only just emerged was but one of many, as I could discern at least two others at irregular distances and varying heights along the gently curving cavern wall before it faded into the misty distance. The sky above me seemed filled with atmospheric nebulae of the same bluish light-vapor that had illuminated my way in the tunnel. It masked the cave ceiling far above, but the latter was probably too high to be seen anyway.

Turning to the level plain below me, I was relieved to see a winding road which eventually led to the tunnel mouth where I stood. In the other direction, I was shocked to see the outcropping clusters of villages and towns. Most of these lined the banks of a serpentine river, crossed and recrossed far more often than seemed necessary by a thousand basalt bridges of elaborate design. These I must examine more closely.

As I made my way carefully down the rubble-choked path, my eyes found it easier to focus. It immediately became evident that the place was populated—or had been. I did not at first see the bodies (numerous though they were) because, upon examination, they seemed to be somehow translucent, suggesting the ghostly likeness of certain deep-sea creatures. Some seemed oddly unstable, as if their tissues had begun to sublimate directly into the air. Needless to say, I had never seen anything like it. Who had?

I examined the clothing of several. The garments were marvelously well-preserved—but then I had no firm reason to believe them ancient, or even old. Most wore tunics or robes which seemed strikingly reminiscent of both Aztec and Greek designs. I shook my head, knowing that here I had found such evidence as every scholar half-dreads: that which threatens to reshuffle the whole deck of cards, to destroy the conventional picture of cultural evolution. But a more immediately puzzling question presented itself. What had happened to these people? I saw nothing living in all the miles I walked, tireless with wonder and dread. I made for a large city in the distance. I guessed it must be this place to which Gray Eagle had sought to direct me, since the specified way of ingress had probably brought me closer to the city than any of the other tunnels would have. Perhaps my answers, about the fallen race as well as the deceased Gray Eagle, lay there.

I passed a great number of the supine, translucent forms, so many that I soon lost count. All of them seemed to be fleeing from some menace, though the positions of some suggested desperate confusion, as if the poor wretches sensed the futility of their flight. As if there were no safety to be had in the whole of their underground world.

As the walls of the city, the name of which I would soon learn to be "Tsath," loomed up before me, my eyes were drawn by the huge sculpted bas reliefs flanking the great city gates. The two great images faced one another, whether in menace or in friendly embrace, I could not tell, since the aspect of both was so alien as to be unreadable. On the left was an octopus-headed titan which seemed to lumber slowly forward to meet its neighbor. The image on the right was that of a vast serpent, coiled in an elaborate, almost Celtic-looking basket interweave. Mighty fangs, more like tusks, curved like sabers from the wide mouth, and scales shaded into feathers in a ridge or fringe along the creature's spine. I hesitated before passing through the portals into the city, half-fancying that the two carven behemoths might be alive, remaining motionless in order to rush together and crush me to a pulp as I passed.

But enter I did, finding none but the dead and disintegrating to keep me company. Building after building had been carved or painted with murals mutely charading an ancient and horrific mythology. I could find evidence of no gods anywhere. All the figures depicted, when not plainly representing the perished underground race, were devils and leviathans, each more hideous than the last. Were any of these terrible figures supposed to be the gods of the subterranean race? Or had they worshipped nothing but devils? It was not a pleasant thing to contemplate—but then neither was the prospect of what it must have taken to send these monster-worshippers bolting into panic!

At length I began to associate most of the recurring images with aspects of the remarkable lore once taught me by Gray Eagle. He had spoken of certain matters only in evocative hints, but the clues were clear enough in view of what I now saw. I concluded that the octopus titan must be none other than the fantastic Tulu, who had first shepherded primordial humanity to the earth where they reigned in the Kingdom called Kuen-Yian. The other being, the snake-creature, must be Yig, the Rattler-King, prototype of Quetzalcoatl and the Hydra. Others were probably to be identified with the deities Nug, Yeb and Nigguratl. Often these figures were shown mounted upon the rampant forms of lean and rangy beasts I knew must represent the dreaded Yith-Hounds. The names and their frightful tales were familiar from the arcane teachings of Gray Eagle, but even their forms were known to me, first-hand, from the visionary journeys upon which I had embarked into the intermediary realms between this world and the next. There I had beheld the frightful forms of the Wrathful Deities. I had never thought to see their effigies in this world.

And then, as I traversed a shadowy avenue of the great mausoleum-city, my eyes fell upon something else whose image I had never expected to behold again on earth: the wizened form of *Gray Eagle*. There he sat in the shadows, whispering so softly that I must have been only subliminally aware of the sound when I turned at no apparent provocation to spy the form of my teacher. He sat, cross-legged, in the drifting shadow, as if the darkness were only a greater thickness of the ubiquitous blue vapor. I hastened to bow to the pavement before the figure, scarcely able to believe what I was seeing. Like the dumbfounded disciples in the gospel accounts, I was speechless before my restored Master. I knew no words from me were required. I waited for him to speak.

When it came, the voice shook with the weight of unnumbered decades. It wavered more than I was accustomed to. There was also a strange tone as of buzzing or hissing in the otherwise familiar voice. But who could calculate the effects of such acoustics as prevailed here? At any rate, I gave little thought to the matter as I strained to catch every revelatory sylla-ble. I will not reproduce verbatim what he said to me, though I believe I could, because some secrets are not good for mankind to know. What I will vouchsafe, though it will sound outlandish enough, was, believe me, merely the outermost fringes of the terrible secrets I heard that day.

The old shaman had a tale to tell surpassing the most extravagant legends he had ever regaled me with in years past. And it concerned the devastation of this, the underground world of Kuen-Yian, where scented gardens no longer bloomed, where the echoes of silver bells on the wind were no longer to be heard.

The cavern-world's history receded back into remote antiquity and unto far-flung worlds of madness. The myths of Tulu bringing the race's progenitors to the new-formed earth were true enough, though the inter-galactic journey was not made in physical form. The adepts of Kuen-Yian had long-ago mastered the art of mind-projection. It was in this incorpo-real form that a group of them had joined Great Tulu on his slow, winging pilgrimage to this world. Upon their advent they displaced the minds of a primitive hominid race which, from what I gathered from Gray Eagle's sketchy description, must have been rather below the level of Neanderthal. The humanoid form took a bit of getting used to, but no doubt it was easier than the adjustment required of the poor primitive earthmen who now found themselves possessed of the original bodies of their usurpers: great, segmented millipedes. Ironically, the poor devils were doubtless as con-fused by the advanced technology of which they could make no use as by the primitive-seeming bodies they wore.

Once ensconced in their new domain, the dwellers in Kuen-Yian eventually grew uneasy with the confines of the underground world. They feared the surface world, always expecting a new wave of extraterrestrial colonizers like themselves, some variety of intelligent crustaceans (I real-ize my narrative only grows more implausible, and that I may well have lost any reader before now!). At an earlier stage, barely mentioned by Gray Eagle in his urgency, the men of Kuen-Yian must have suffered terrible losses in conflict with these "space devils." So when the lust for conquest struck them, they turned their attentions *downward*, to other, deeper cavern worlds of which they had become aware. Below the blue-lit world, it seemed, there lay another, filled with red radiance, this one called "Yoth." And below this there yawned a lightless abyss called N'Kai, the ancient lair of the polar deity Tsathoggua. My mind was by now spinning with the knowledge of worlds within worlds and unknown universes beyond.

To conquer the reptilian denizens of the Yoth-world was a simple matter for beings with the psychic talents of Kuen-Yian. After the use of clairvoyant powers for reconnaissance, they would first assign the appropriate number of their own men to enter a fortified retention zone, then have them concentrate on those below, exchanging minds with the Yothians for long enough to place the latter's minds in their own incarcerated bodies. Then, wearing the scaly bodies of their captives, they would make their way to their own level and perform the soul-projection in reverse. It was a bloodless, yet entirely effective, maneuver. And yet perhaps the victory was not so definitive as it first seemed. One of the elder sages of Yoth had silently vowed revenge.

I had it in mind to interrupt to ask how on earth Gray Eagle could possibly have known such details as the inner thoughts of a member of a vanished alien species. Despite my years of confidence in the old man, my own faith in him was beginning to slip. I had accepted a great many outrageous assertions up to now, but I found myself listening as to a fictional tale (just as you, reader, must feel perusing my own).

The shaman, as he always had, knew my thoughts before I could voice them. And his answer to my implicit query was even more fantastic. Nonetheless, certain things began to fall into place, his astounding longevity, for instance. I had attributed his remarkable span in some vague manner to his occult disciplines, his knowledge of obscure herbs and medicaments. But this hypothesis I had never dared examine too closely. I suppose I had feared to hear something like this. Gray Eagle was no Indian. Instead he was none other than the captive Yothian elder himself. And his moment of vengeance finally came.

Signs of the religious preoccupation of the men of Kuen-Yian were everywhere, especially of the cults of Tulu and Yig, as I have said. Over the centuries, Gray Eagle recounted, the people had progressed from a literal belief in these deities (which Gray Eagle himself seemed to share) to a more philosophical creed in which Great Tulu and Father Yig had become allegories for various natural forces and ideal principles, much in the manner of the Stoic abstraction of lusty Zeus into the pantheistic Logos. This was followed in turn by a period of decadent *ennui* in which the more venturesome of Kuen-Yian experimented in a playful way with the old rites of Tulu and Tsathoggua. Gray Eagle saw all these developments, since he had been one of the elite among the Yoth-prisoners eventually to be received freely into the Kuen-Yian society, as occasional venturers from above or below had been for several centuries. And he knew well what the people of Kuen-Yian had forgotten. These were no games they were playing. Consulting the ancient Yoth manuscripts plundered from below only served to confirm his fears, for he knew that the time was nearing when the constellations would assume once again their ancient configurations heralding the glorious return of the sleeping Tulu. He more than half-suspected that it was the subtle influence of the stirring god that had awakened in the frivolous worshippers the peculiar desire to adopt the mummery of the old faith. And if Tulu should arise, the world would fall, both the world above and that below.

Though Gray Eagle had no love for those whom he still regarded as his captors, he resolved to turn them from this disastrous course. He was willing to share the world with even those of Kuen-Yian as long as there remained a world to share. He wasted no time in trying to convince any of the rulers; he knew he could expect naught but rude incredulity. So he returned to the study of the old Yothian scrolls, at last concluding that his only hope to stop the blasphemous consummation lay in an equally perilous move. He would summon the entity, N-Yog-tha, the dweller in the deep fissures of the earth. He was the last and the mightiest of the vanished race of N'Kai who had in ancient days retreated below to unguessed chasms. He might be summoned to wreak havoc among one's enemies, as the dubious myths of Yoth related. Gray Eagle would invoke him secretly while feigning participation in the Tulu rites. The ensuing chaos should end the dangerous liturgies. And if somehow Tulu made his appearance anyway, if things had already gone too far to be stopped, why then, it might be that the two titans would meet in battle and annihilate one another.

Gray Eagle went ahead with his plans, and the results were still manifest. It was in flight from the rampaging N-Yog-tha that the doomed dwellers of Kuen-Yian met their terrible deaths, as I myself had seen. All this had happened generations ago. At that time Gray Eagle had taken the opportunity to escape the ruins of Kuen-Yian and gain his first look at the surface world. There he had experienced little difficulty in taking a place among one of the Oklahoma Indian tribes. Changing his appearance, whether in reality or by hypnotic illusion, he took the name Gray Eagle and became a shaman and hierophant of the cult of Yig. He achieved great fame among his adopted people in the nineteenth century during the last stages of the U.S. government's take-over of Indian territories. Determined not to see the White man treat his adopted countrymen as the men of Kuen-Yian had dealt with his own people of Yoth, Gray Eagle became the leader of one of the smaller Ghost Dance movements who sought to turn back the invaders by magical means. Of course these efforts failed, at least the ones chronicled in the history books. But there was one unaccounted clash in which an entire detachment of U.S. Cavalry had simply vanished as far as anyone knew.

He lived thus in self-imposed exile for many years, an object of curiosity among frontier villagers and of tremendous veneration among Indians. All was well, if uneventful, as he rested content in the assumption that he had prevented the impending advent of monstrous Tulu.

But only months ago the old man's tranquility had been shattered by some arcane intimation that the appearance of Great Tulu had only been delayed, not stymied. The glacial progress of the turning stars allowed plenty of time, and now the time was near. Gray Eagle had returned to Kuen-Yian to wait and see what would transpire. His occult powers had grown much since his escape from Kuen-Yian, but he doubted they would be of any real use in preventing Tulu's return. What he planned, if anything, he would not tell me. I wondered if he planned again to summon N-Yog-tha, but he would say nothing either to confirm or deny the suggestion. Why then had he called me here?

The old man was silent, as if not sure how much to explain to me. Finally he spoke. His intention was that, in the event that Great Tulu were to be freed to ravage the earth, someone should escape the general dissolution to carry the knowledge of past ages into whatever future might someday evolve. I should be that messenger. But how?

Gray Eagle had managed to learn something of the astral time-voyaging practiced to such great effect by the men of Kuen-Yian. It was by these techniques, combined with his own Yothian clairvoyant and hypnotic abilities, that he had eventually discovered that the Kuen-Yian inhabitants had not really perished but managed to project their minds forward into the bodies of a far-future race. But they had found their new physical forms and environment (much more like those of their own ancient home across the galaxy) so amenable that they quickly settled into the familiar existence and actually came to forget their unearthly origins, claiming the heritage of the future race as their own history. And Gray Eagle, who had both seen and made so much history, could not bear that a whole planet should sink into lazy amnesia. He knew me for a scholar and a teacher who could not deny such an opportunity as he now offered me. He knew me well.

My old mentor began to emerge from the murk of the shadow-mists, revealing a heavily beaded and mottled reptilian hide where before his powers of mesmerism had caused the image of a lined Indian face to appear. I had ceased to doubt his story, even though it had only become more extravagant as it lengthened. But now there was proof positive of his wild tales. I gazed upon the sole surviving visage of a reptile-man of hidden Yoth.

His hand reached for me with serpentine ease and rested with an icy touch upon my forehead. He continued to speak, but not in audible sounds. His thoughts appeared directly in my mind, in my memory, as if he were reawakening dormant recollections, something like *déjà vu*. At any rate, I shortly knew what I had to do to make the jump. Like Lot, I took no time to consider what I was leaving behind, of what might be destroyed by an impending cataclysm. Gray Eagle allowed me no more time than was necessary to pen the narrative you are now reading. It was, I supposed, another attempt at preserving knowledge of the past in case my mission should fail, or perhaps to corroborate it should that be needful. From here on in I can only look toward the future—and try to enter into it.

Here the inscribed sheets ended their peculiar story. It was not easy for him to roll them up and insert them back into the cylinder. So he left that for the archivists. Zkafka was one of the scholar gentry of the great insectoid civilization thriving on a strange earth with all her continents rejoined. Now he turned his eight facet-eyes away to survey his own chitinous form, as if suddenly seeing it in a new light. He had somehow known that one day the manuscript would surface. It had, and he had read it. Now he was certain, terribly certain, that the peculiar dreams of a past existence in the form of a hairy biped called "man" were no mere dreams, but memories. It was all true; that he could no longer doubt, since one of the most disturbing dreams had been that of writing this very manuscript.

Part Two: The Trial
by Peter Cannon

ZKAFKA SKITTERED OUT OF ARCHIVAL HALL as fast as his eleven pairs of legs could take him. His burrow was only about a hundred body lengths away, but he had barely gone a tenth of that distance when two secret police coleoptera scuttled up on either side and seized him by the antennae. Resistance was futile. They marched him directly to police headquarters, where he was taken before the duty officer.

"With what crime is this individual charged?" the duty officer asked.
"Blasphemy, sir," answered one of the coleoptera.

"Blasphemy! When will these heretics ever learn? Better shut him in the lowest level of the dungeon."

In the endless days that followed Zkafka had ample opportunity to reflect on the nature of his *crime*. What it boiled down to was this: He couldn't be sure just how old the cylinder and manuscript were, but from his dreams he knew that they dated back at least a hundred million years, when the land was broken into several large continental masses. The problem was that the holy book of the coleopterous race taught that the earth, along with the entire universe, was created by Superbeetle a mere twelve thousand years ago. Any *evidence* of an older earth was the work of Superbeetle's enemies, the Saucers from Yaddith, planted to mislead the more gullible among them—who more often than not were members of the scholar gentry, like Zkafka. Not that Zkafka would have said or done anything to challenge the prevailing orthodoxy, but unfortunately, it was sufficient that he held *incorrect thoughts* to merit his present predicament.

On the face of it be had to admit the authorities had an excellent case against him. Contrary to what the manuscript implied, time travel was a feat far beyond the capacities of the coleoptera, who, despite their self-proclaimed *greatness,* had developed only the most primitive technology. In truth, their body forms ill suited them for even the simplest of mechanical tasks, like screwing off lids. Digging holes in the ground was about all at which they could claim to excel—and even this had led to trouble with the unearthing of so-called fossils of extinct life forms and the bushels of blue-gray metal cylinders with their impossible narratives, collected and catalogued at Archival Hall.

Once a day a guard rolled back the stone that blocked his pitch-black cell and regurgitated a load of half-digested leaves and grasses that constituted his daily diet.

Every other day a fibrous tube was stuck through a small air hole and a noxious chemical sprayed into the cell. A non-lethal dose, it left him too weak to attempt to dig his way through the frangible limestone walls of his prison. Iron shackles and chains were unknown to the coleoptera, with their utter ignorance of metallurgy.

One morning (not that he could really tell it was morning), Zkafka woke up from a deep sleep full of dreams of feathered snakes and quaint cavern-worlds to discover that he had company. Nestled along the length of his carapace was a living creature—another coleopteron judging from the feel of the scuta. There wasn't a lot of room to maneuver.

Zkafka tried to roll over, but for his pains he got twelve or fourteen of his legs entangled with a corresponding number of the intruder's appendages.

"Awfully sorry, old bug," said the newcomer in a cultivated tone that marked him as belonging to the scholar gentry. "I didn't ask to be stuck in this hole, you know."

"No more than I did, I'm sure," said Zkafka. "Are you in here by chance for—"

"Yes, for blasphemy, Yig damn it!"

Once they'd sorted out their body parts and curled up as best they could to minimize physical contact, the two agreed to swap stories. Since he'd been jailed much longer, Zkafka went first. To the stranger, who introduced himself as Kzweig, he related the substance of his dreams—of his discovery of a blue-lit subterranean world called Kuen-Yian; of his forays into red-lit Yoth and lightless N'Kai; of his unwitting worship of Tulu and Tsathoggua and their brethren; and finally of Gray Eagle, his wise and wily mentor, who had passed among the humans indigenous to the region of the surface world known as Oklahoma but who was in fact the leader of the squamous-skinned Yothians—and who possessed the immemorial secret of astral time-voyaging.

"In sum, based on my dreams and what I apparently recorded about a hundred million years ago," said Zkafka, "I expected to find myself today among the men, now insects, of Kuen-Yian—in other words, amidst enlightened friends, not superstitious savages!"

Kzweig didn't immediately respond. In the darkness, as seconds stretched into minutes, Zkafka began to wonder if he'd been too open in his eagerness to communicate.

Perhaps his cell-mate was not an innocent victim like himself but a police spy sent to betray him. Three of his eyes started to itch, but he was too tense to move.

At last his companion spoke: "Forgive me, old bug, your tale is deeply affecting, but I had to decide whether I could trust you or not before I replied. Can't be too careful what you say to whom in a place like this."

"My sentiments exactly," said Zkafka, rubbing his eye facets in relief.

"I've looked into dozens of cases similar to yours," continued Kzweig. "I'm a psychologist, a specialist in alien abductions. Initially I was convinced that a sinister plot or possibly mass delusion explained the metal cylinders and their disquieting contents.

"Eventually, however, I could no longer deny reality. I had to conclude that these artifacts were ancient, vastly older than the alpha point which the powers-that-be hold sacred. I could not conceal my new understanding. I was soon picked up.

"Your account confirms that the natives of Kuen-Yian migrated across the eons, exchanging minds with the more sensitive and intelligent types of the present era. A pity someone miscalculated, for the Kuen-Yians' numbers were few in proportion to those of the prolific coleoptera. Not only that, the beetle civilization proved to be considerably less advanced than their own—to be blunt, rather barbaric. I guess I don't have to tell you that the police take a dim view of these migrant souls once they've been identified."

It was Zkafka's turn to ponder in silence. He was too proud to admit he was confused, not to mention a bit dismayed. After all, in his past life he had been a hairy carnivorous biped, not a member of the superior Kuen-Yian race. Given his lowly status, why had he been transported through time—and by whom? Was he unique—or had other human beings as well as other lesser life forms suffered the same fate?

Maybe his new friend had some of the answers, but before Zkafka could resume the conversation an acrid chemical mist flooded the cell, more potent than any previous assault to his scent sensors. As his consciousness began to fade, he heard Kzweig chitter, "Don't despair, old bug. Keep a stiff upper mandible."

♦   ♦   ♦

When Zkafka awoke he was nearly blinded by sunlight. He needed to squint through all eight of his eyes in order to take in his surroundings. On either side of him stood two police guards, their claws cocked in dangerous vicinity of his antennae. In front of him, elevated on a flat table-like stone, were several high officials wearing wigs of bushy vegetation that spilled from head to thorax. Zkafka realized he was in a court of law.

Towering behind the table-like stone was a contraption built of reinforced logs topped by a boulder. Three hooded coleoptera lay on an adjacent platform, ready to push. Zkafka suspected that there would be little time between sentencing and execution.

A crowd of spectators, gathered at the fringes in a giant semi-circle, buzzed and droned until one of the officials rose up on his hind legs and called for order. Once the noise subsided, this same official, evidently a clerk, started to read the indictment from a tablet entitled *Coleoptera of Earth versus Zkafka*. Filled with legal jargon, the text was by and large incomprehensible. Zkafka stopped listening after the first minute.

"The prisoner is hereby charged with blasphemy in the first-degree, a violation of section one, article one, paragraph one of the religious code," the clerk at last intoned.

"How does the prisoner plead?"

"Not guilty!" shouted the official in the largest and gaudiest wig, no doubt the judge. "They always plead that way, the arrogant fools. Let's get on with it. Call your first witness, prosecutor."

"Thank you, your honor," said another official. "The court calls as its first witness Zkafka."

"Excuse me, your honor, but do I have to defend myself?" asked Zkafka as the guards prodded him into the packed dirt in front of the table stone.

"Of course. You had more than three moon cycles in the dungeon to consider your own defense."

"Yeah, I suppose."

The clerk administrated the oath. Zkafka lifted five of his right legs and swore to tell the truth *so help me Superbeetle*. The prosecutor slithered down the side of the table stone and joined Zkafka on the ground. In his forelegs he carried an iridescent blue-gray cylinder. It was marked *Beetles' Exhibit A*.

"Have you ever seen this object before?" the prosecutor asked, brandishing the cylinder under Zkafka's mouthparts.

"Possibly. As a scholar at Archival Hall I saw many such cylinders."

"Fine. I'll grant you these cylinders all look alike. However, when it comes to the individual contents . . . let's just have a peek inside, shall we?"

The prosecutor began to attempt to unscrew the top, but it soon became apparent he was having difficulty. Either the catch wasn't working or his claws couldn't get a purchase on the smooth metal. It was some comfort to Zkafka that the prosecution was no better prepared than he was.

"Here, you have a go," said the prosecutor, giving up in exasperation. He tossed the cylinder to Zkafka.

Taken by surprise, Zkafka dropped *Beetles' Exhibit A*. Instinct told him to feign inability even to clasp it, let alone remove the top. "I usually let the archivists take care of opening and closing these things," he mumbled. He hoped his performance was persuasive.

"Here now, that's enough," said the judge impatiently. "Next question."

The prosecutor grabbed the cylinder away from Zkafka's fumbling legs and set it down by a knot of spectators, one of whom proceeded to gnaw on it, with no better results than the others.

"My apologies, your honor," said the prosecutor, still somewhat abashed. "I'll try another tack. Zkafka, when was the world created?"

"The holy book states that the world was created in the year zero, otherwise known as the alpha-point."

"The year zero, otherwise known as the alpha-point. And how long ago was that?"

"Twelve thousand years."

"Twelve thousand years, you say."

"Yes, give or take a century."

"No, that's what the holy book says," cried the prosecutor in triumph. "I want to know how old you, Zkafka, think the earth is."

"Well, that depends," Zkafka responded hesitantly. "My own theory is that everything was made nearly two years ago, complete with memories and signs of a past that never existed."

The prosecutor seemed ready for this flippant answer. "Surely you jest. By that theory everything could have been created any time in the past—like in the last minute or even in the last second."

"Superbeetle works in mysterious ways."

"How dare you take His name in vain, you blasphemer," shrieked the judge. "Next question."

"Zkafka, do you acknowledge Superbeetle as your lord and master?" continued the prosecutor.

"Sure, doesn't everybody?"

"No, I'm afraid not everybody does. There are some misguided coleoptera who owe their allegiance to—*the Saucers from Yaddith.* Ever hear tell of the Saucers from Yaddith?"

"Uh . . . "

"Those insidious spreaders of false doctrine, those cosmic garbage collectors, those organ thieves—is it not true that you, Zkafka, are one of their chief agents on this planet?"

"No! How can I be when the Saucers from Yaddith are only a myth?"

"A myth? You dare call the Saucers from Yaddith a myth?"

"Yes, evil isn't real—it can't exist given Superbeetle's inherent goodness. The Saucers from Yaddith merely represent the dark side of our psyches. They grow out of our own very earthly fears. They're symbols of those fears."

Again, Zkafka felt as if he'd stumped the prosecution. Maybe, just maybe, there was hope he'd be spared after all. In any event, he would fight as best he could to the end.

The prosecutor appeared at a loss. He skittled over to the table stone, where he conducted a lengthy whispered conference with his colleagues on top. One of them gave him two small items Zkafka couldn't see. The prosecutor returned and presented Zkafka with the new evidence, marked *Beetles' Exhibit B* and *Beetles' Exhibit C*. One was a fountain pen, the other a blank sheet of writing paper. He recognized them instantly as manufactured artifacts of the hairy bipeds of the prehistoric past.

As with the metal cylinder, it was clear the prosecutor was hoping to get Zkafka to show some familiarity with the use of these arcane objects (literate coleoptera wrote with their claws on wet clay). Zkafka saw no point in pretending to be unable to hold the pen, however awkward it was to do so, for the ink had long dried up and the fragile paper easily tore. An impartial observer would have deemed this demonstration another fiasco for the prosecution. Alas, there was no impartial observer in the court.

Undaunted, the prosecutor called his next witness—Kzweig. Zkafka remained where he was while the crowd parted to allow his erstwhile cell-mate, escorted by two guards, to approach the table stone. The clerk started to administer the oath. At first Kzweig raised his left legs then the wrong number of right legs before he got it straight. None of his eyes would meet any of Zkafka's eyes.

"Kzweig, what is your profession?" asked the prosecutor.

"I'm a psychologist."

"As a psychologist, do you have a specialty?"

"Yes, I'm an expert on alien abduction cases."

"Have you had an opportunity to examine the defendant, Zkafka?"

"No, not in a strictly professional sense."

"In what sense then?"

"We did recently share a prison cell . . . "

"Prison cells tend to be on the small side, don't they?"

"Objection, your honor!" cried Zkafka. "The prosecutor is asking the witness to express an opinion."

"Whether the prosecutor is asking the witness to express an opinion or to state a fact," replied the judge, "is, in the view of the court, a matter of opinion." This display of wit provoked more than a few chuckles and guffaws from the assembly. "Witness must answer the question."

"Your honor," interjected the prosecutor, "may I ask another question instead?"

The judge nodded, causing his wig to slip. Everyone waited respectfully until he had adjusted it.

"Kzweig," the prosecutor resumed, "as a result of sharing a tiny cell with the defendant you couldn't help becoming intimate, is that not so?"

"Yes."

"You exchanged confidences?"

"It was the natural thing to do."

"Did Zkafka tell you that he was a spy in the pay of the Saucers from Yaddith?'

"Objection!" yelled Zkafka.

"Overruled," said the judge.

There was a pause while Kzweig shuffled from one set of legs to another. He kept all his eyes fixed on the ground.

"You must answer the question," said the judge with some asperity, addressing Kzweig. "And remember, your freedom depends on how you reply."

"Could you repeat the question?"

"Did the defendant, with whom you shared a *cramped* cell, tell you that he was a spy in the pay of the Saucers from Yaddith?" said the prosecutor, enunciating every word.

At this point Kzweig started a slow shuffle. He lifted alternate legs higher and higher and faster and faster—he was doing a jig. Zkafka felt the air vibrate. The sunlight shimmered.

"Are you insane?" barked the judge. "Stop that dancing at once!"

Kzweig didn't stop until the pair of guards, at a signal from the judge, seized him by the antennae, which they twisted sharply. Other guards rushed over and stabbed his exoskeleton with the points of their claws. It wasn't long before the court had obtained the answer from the witness they'd been expecting to hear in the first place.

"That concludes our case, your honor," said the prosecutor.

"Very good. The court will now retire to deliberate."

"Wait a minute, your honor," wailed Zkafka, "don't I get a chance to state my side of the case? You yourself questioned the sanity of the last witness—"

"Silence! Do you wish the guards to discipline you also?"

This seemed rather an absurd threat in the circumstances, but Zkafka decided it was useless to protest further. By now he was meekly resigned to his fate.

The judge and the other officials huddled briefly on the table stone. The clerk picked up a tablet, evidently a prepared text, and read the verdict: "The court finds the accused, Zkafka, guilty as charged of blasphemy in the first degree."

"You are hereby condemned," cried the judge, "to be squashed!"

A phalanx of guards formed around Zkafka, who had no choice but to follow along as they commenced to march around the table stone, toward the place of execution. At one point he stepped slightly aside to avoid a puddle on the path.

When they reached the tower, the guards each seized two or three of Zkafka's legs and stretched him out over the target area. Above, at the top of the tower, half his eyes could see the boulder shifting closer to the edge. With the other half of his eyes he noticed Kzweig, ignored and off by himself, engaged in more frenzied dancing. Again the sunlight shimmered. Then Kzweig lunged past the crowd and threw himself on top of Zkafka, like a mother sacrificing her own life in a seemingly futile effort to save the life of her young. Only one eye, the rest being blocked by the body of his friend, saw the boulder fall . . .

♦   ♦   ♦

In the next instant Zkafka was soaring and plunging through the void. Viscous, uncouth clouds of vapor, loaded with whirring, bladder-shaped disks, swirled around him like chocolate chips and cookie dough in a blender. Was he dead, his soul streaking into limbo? No, he had somehow survived, for traveling next to him was Kzweig—with whom he discovered he could communicate telepathically.

"My apologies, old bug, that was a close call!" his companion's brain waves informed him. "It took me a lot longer to get the ether vibrating than I expected. Guess I was nervous."

"Why didn't you rescue us in the dungeon?" Zkafka relayed with some asperity.

"I had to make sure you were who you claimed you were. Believe me, I was all set to break into the phantom zone from our prison, but then we got sprayed. I did my best to stall at the trial."

It suddenly struck Zkafka that Kzweig was more than he claimed to be.

"Who are you?" he transmitted.

"Why, haven't you figured it out? I'm your old guide and counselor— Gray Eagle."

"Gray Eagle!"

"My landing in the body of a psychologist was both a blessing and curse, believe me."

"If you're Gray Eagle, then that means we're headed . . . "

"Yes, back in time more than a hundred million years—to Binger, Oklahoma, during the early part of what the surface folk called the twentieth century."

"In order to . . . "

"Yes, it was I who miscalculated. It was I who talked the men of Kuen-Yian into migrating en masse into the bodies of the coleopterous race, only to meet their collective doom. I think if I could start over again I can undo the damage."

"Can my mind take over the body of one of the Kuen-Yians this round? I'd prefer not to be human."

Before Gray Eagle could answer, the viscous clouds abruptly condensed, the whirring disks caressed their carcasses like electric buffers, and they were rushing and tearing downward like jet pilots in free-fall. Zkafka blacked out.

♦   ♦   ♦

When Zkafka regained consciousness, he discovered they were on an empty country road, surrounded by high hedges and lush green trees. It was raining lightly. A signpost read *Brichester 6 miles* and underneath *Warrendown 1 mile.*

"This terrain and climate just don't seem right for Oklahoma," said his mentor. "In my haste I may have steered us a little off course, but I'm pretty confident we're okay time-wise."

A motor vehicle was approaching them from up the road. It was slowing down. Then it hit him (the delicacy of their situation, not the car).

"Kzweig, I mean Gray Eagle, you're still in your coleopterous body!" moaned Zkafka.

"Sorry to disappoint you, old bug, but so are you . . . "

Part Three: The Horror at the Lake
by Donald R. Burleson

THE SEVERN VALLEY HADN'T CHANGED AT ALL—it was still spectral, still gloomy, still darkly steeped (no doubt) in morbid folklore; nor had he expected it to change, or wanted it to. Edging his car along the road to Brichester, Khem-Bei Ramses reflected that as the most popular writer of horror fiction in England, he scarcely even needed to embellish this ghastly place in order to set his disturbing and fantastic tales here, when the very terrain seemed redolent of horror.

The region beyond Brichester would always be the strangest, but even here, where great gnarled trees stood over-arching the road like malevolent sentries, the effect was grim; and even though the light rain was stopping, so little daylight filtered through the foliage that he had to squint at the shadowy turnings and windings of the road ahead, and when he saw what he saw, the impression was far from clear.

He instinctively slowed the car (though on this ill-paved road he had already been driving slowly) and peered into the dappled shadows further along, but whatever it might have been that he had seen, it was gone now.

He could have sworn that it looked for all the world like two large, black insects—shiny and carapaced, like beetles—scurrying off the road into the woods to his right, disappearing into the dense stand of patriarchal trees just before he could get a good look.

It must have been an illusion, of course, a trick of the uncertain light. Then again, in the Severn Valley one had to grow accustomed to unaccountable things, it seemed. How often had he used the unadorned strangeness of the Gloucestershire region to hint at dark and brooding horrors in his fiction?

But the fleeting impression he had had, just now, left him feeling especially moved somehow, as if there were something, some strain of lore that he should remember, but could not.

When he got into Brichester, with its moss-encrusted inn, its narrow winding lanes and solemn university towers, he stopped at the inn only long enough to drop his baggage off in his upstairs room. Leaving the car parked at the inn, he walked across town to the university library, where he soon tracked down someone whose help he had often relied upon before in his arcane quests.

"Mei-Ling, it's good to see you again."

The librarian, attractive but almost stereotypically inscrutable, nodded. "And you, Mr. Ramses. Have you come to do some more research?"

"Well," Ramses said, "I hadn't planned on anything very extensive this time, Mei-Ling, but something has come up and I do need to consult—you know."

The woman's eyes seemed to retreat a little into a formidable little nest of judgment. "Not *The Revelations of Glaaki*?"

'Yes, I'm afraid so," Ramses admitted. "I don't mean to impose on you—"

"But you know very well that the Trustees decidedly frown upon anyone's—" She stopped, evidently reassessing the expression on his face, and sighed deeply. "Oh, very well. I suppose one can make an exception in your case. You *have* consulted the *Glaaki* before."

She took him through the hush of the library to the Special Collections Room, where she closed and locked the door behind them and switched on the lights. There, in a padlocked glass-topped display case, lay the great mouldy volumes in question.

"I shall leave you to your studies," the librarian said, unlocking the case, whose contents she eyed with obvious distaste. "Just press the buzzer when you wish me to return. And remember, we close at ten."

Alone with the ill-regarded tomes, Ramses took one ponderous volume at a time to the reading table, searching among them for the right passage, the faint memory, the nearly forgotten reference that persisted in haunting some back corner of his mind. He had looked through nearly all the volumes and was beginning to think the elusive memory a shred of self-delusion, when suddenly he came upon what he sought.

"'The wisdom of Glaaki encompasses many things,'" he read aloud to the shadowy room. "'From times sunken in frightful antiquity, to those times, dizzyingly far-flung into the mists of futurity, times that are not yet but must someday be—indeed of all of time, the wisdom of Glaaki speaks to the minds of those who worship Him. Of times old beyond memory, of future times beyond imagining, it is chronicled, in the Zkafka Manuscript—'"

And he read, again, more carefully this time, a remarkable account whose details he had only skimmed once before. He read of great Tulu, or Hlu-Hlu, who had oozed down from the icy stars bringing proto-human-kind to earth; he read of the races that once dwelt in cavernous regions beneath a mound in Oklahoma, including the men of blue-litten Kuen-Yian and, beneath them but not so far down as the horrors of blackest N'Kai, the reptilian denizens of red-litten Yoth, one of whom, captured and confined in Kuen-Yian, later passed himself off above ground as an American Indian sage named Gray Eagle and projected himself and one other forward, mentally, to a stupendously distant time when the similarly projected men of Kuen-Yian lived in the bodies of great coleopterous be-ings but knew not their ancient origins. Gray Eagle and his human com-panion Zkafka, lodged likewise in coleopterous bodies, would travel back in time and encounter yet further mysteries.

"'And there would come a time,'" Khem-Bei Ramses intoned from the musty pages of *The Revelations of Glaaki*, "'when such forces would con-verge that all would be confounded.'"

That was all. Closing the book with a thud that echoed unpleasantly in the dreary room, Ramses thought: coleoptera. Beetles.

Large, black beetles, such as what he thought he had glimpsed on the road?

Good heavens, could it be?

As a writer of the macabre, he had often made use of *The Revelations of Glaaki* as a fictional prop, but he had never been sure whether this multi-volume grimoire might not encompass, in the extravagance of its claims, some obscure residuum of truth.

Could it be that the account of great coleopterous beings inhabiting the earth of the future might be more than fantasy? Could it be that he himself had seen travelers from that mythically distant age, when the shapes that roamed the earth—but what would they be doing here? There could be no reason for their being here.

Unless, perhaps, in some arcane manner this perpetually strange region, so immersed in bizarre lore, had had a way of *attracting* such visitors. What any of it meant, he could scarcely guess. For now, he pressed the buzzer, bringing the vaguely disapproving but polite Mei-Ling, and thanked her and left the library, walking back across the university quadrangle and down the street to his inn. By now it was quite late, and he was dead tired.

But in his little room at the inn, his sleep was disturbed by strange dreams. He thought vile insectoid shapes gathered before him, thrusting their angular visages into his own face and speaking to him, speaking of the imminent appearance of Great Tulu, back again from untold depths. *Tu-lu, Tu-lu, Tu-lu*: the primordial sound that was not a sound echoed phantasmally in his skull like some frightful omen. And as he listened to the buzzing speech of the beetle-creatures, another form, vast and hideous, rose near him, as if from some dark body of water, and he awoke, sweating profusely, shivering.

Tossing and writhing in his bed then till past midnight, he finally gave up the effort to get back to sleep. He got up and dressed himself, and slipped quietly down the stairs and through the lobby and out the door, into the night, barely pausing to think where he was going, or why, until he found himself driving out of town into the tenebrous region beyond Brichester.

He was heading, he suddenly realized, toward the lake.

It was one of the most evilly-regarded places in all the Severn River Valley, this sombre lake with its decrepit row of old three-story wood-frame houses standing, but only just barely standing, on an odd little cobblestone lane beside the water. It was in these houses, he recalled, that there had dwelt the furtive cult whose members had penned the infamous *Revelations*, around the notion of a timeless and unspeakable thing that lived in the lake, an abominable creature whom the cult worshipped with a fervor hideous, by all accounts, to behold. Now the cult was long since vanished and the houses were little more than windy shells, yet stories of disappearances and possible sacrifices circulated from time to time, and the legend of Glaaki was far from dead. The authorities, in frustration, had even spoken of draining the lake one day to dispel its awful mystique and prove once and for all that nothing lived beneath the noisome waters.

But at times Khem-Bei Ramses half believed that Glaaki, the Inhabitant of the Lake, was real.

"Or is it just wishful thinking, old bean?" he asked himself as the car nosed its tentative way along the increasingly primitive road, headlights probing the palpable darkness ahead like pale ineffectual fingers. "You'd love to believe, wouldn't you, that something lives in the lake?"

The car came around a sharp curve to the right, and he could have sworn that among the jittering shadows frightened into motion by the headlamps, something large and dark scuttled away into the cover of the trees. It might have been only an effect of the erratic light, but something about the way the thing appeared to move made his skin crawl. He gripped the steering wheel more tightly and slowed nearly to a stop, passing the spot where he thought he had seen something; but now he saw only dense, brooding woods. And all at once he understood why he would love to believe that something lived in the lake—some godlike entity from which one might learn profound and unthinkable things. The dark, fathomless woods beside the road suddenly struck him as a metaphor for ignorance, for potential depths of knowledge into which one could scarcely hope to penetrate, unless—

At length the car emerged from beneath the overhanging trees, pulling into a relatively open area, where to his right a ragged row of six gaunt, half-fallen houses leaned like rotten teeth along the gumline of a little cobblestone street under the pallid radiance of a gibbous moon just climbing beyond the dark backdrop of trees; and to his left, the sable waters of the lake itself gave back a sickly reflection of moonlight.

He stopped the car just short of the cobblestones, turned off the engine and the headlights, and got out and walked a little distance along the street, pausing in front of the third house, whose outlines, though half collapsed, were more nearly intact than the others. During past visits here—by daylight—he had explored these ruined houses, but having no desire to do so now, he turned and stepped closer to the lake, whose unguent waters he watched with a growing sense of purpose. Finally he spoke, a little startled at the sound, out here, all alone of his own voice.

"Is it true, then? Is there an Inhabitant of the Lake?'"

The waters only whispered incoherently. An undulating ribbon of pale moonglow ran out over the surface of the lake like a phosphorescent tongue, and a light breath of wind brought a subtle froth of quiet waves closer to his feet. He spoke again, feeling somewhat foolish.

"Glaaki, Eternal One, I believe in You."

Somehow the words, once they were out on the air, didn't sound so foolish after all. And he recalled the requisite incantation; he had read it in the vile tomes at the university library, and he well remembered that the same incantation was written, apparently in blood, on the crumbling walls inside one of the houses behind him.

"Hear me," he intoned, "O Great One, pause in Your endless voyage through eternity to hear the prayers of one who would humbly worship You. From the aeons, from the waters, from the fever-ridden folds of night, come forth. I call to You, O Glaaki, I invoke You. Primal Glaaki, at whose mention the very stars tremble—come forth."

As his voice died away over the gurgling waters, he stood motionless, listening, but heard only the noncommittal soughing of the wind.

No, there was another sound—not out in front of him, not from the lake, but from somewhere behind him.

Turning around, he squinted into the gloomy space between two of the ramshackle houses, a corridor of black where the feeble rays of the moon didn't quite reach. He thought he saw something moving there.

After a moment he was certain that he had seen something, because it was advancing out into the moonlight, coming slowly toward him. It was—unmistakably, undeniably—a large black beetle, somewhat longer than an average man was tall, and its unacceptably many feet clacked on the cobblestones as it moved closer. And behind it, likewise scrabbling loathsomely across the stones, came another.

He was about to fling himself backward into the water, when two things stopped him. The first thing was that the coleopterous shapes halted a few feet away from him and appeared disinclined to advance farther. The second thing was that the waters behind him were beginning to churn and seethe, as if something large were stirring them.

But now the great black beetle nearer to him drew all his attention by raising its head slightly, staring at him with multifaceted eyes and clicking its mandibles. Ramses had the distinct feeling that the thing was trying to *speak* to him, and indeed a buzzing sort of impression, not sound but something mental, filled his head.

I am Gray Eagle, it said, and the sensation, in Ramses' head, carried with it a certain undercurrent of pain.

Behind, the waters sounded more agitated than before, but he dared not turn to look. The beetle-thing in front of him projected another burst of pure thought.

I must occupy your body, it said, and the pain at Ramses' temples returned.

But now the second coleopteron moved up beside the first and projected its own thought, evidently intending it for its fellow beetle, though it flooded Ramses' head as well. *Wait. I mean no disrespect, my old master, but you are originally a denizen of red-litten Yoth, and not human. I am human in my original form and have the more urgent need. Should I not have first choice of a way to leave this abominable shape?*

The pain in Ramses' head increased considerably with this more protracted exchange, but it wasn't over. Behind, the waters were thrashing wildly now, and Ramses had started to turn around to see what was happening, when a new burst of painful mental projection stopped him.

It is my prerogative, my friend Zkafka, to choose, and I insist that I must occupy this human form for the return to Kuen Yian, beneath the sands of western Oklahoma, a return that will not misfire this time. When I have returned there I shall reach out and pull your mind into a convenient host. But I must have my host first; I cannot continue to occupy this detestable form. More importantly, the need to return to the Great Mound is urgent. The reappearance of Tulu is imminent. The stars have come 'round right. If Tulu rises without the opposition of whatever deterring influences may be brought to bear . . .

By now the pain in Ramses' skull was hideous, and his nose had begun to bleed. The disagreement was evidently going to continue; the Zkafka-beetle was offering some rejoinder when the noise—and now the smell—from the lake grew truly appalling, and Ramses had to turn around and look.

What had risen from the black frothy waters was enough to shock him nearly senseless. It was a great pulpy thing with ragged appendages like fins, and its bulging eyes were so far apart that it took Ramses a moment to realize that he was looking into some diseased excuse for a face, in which a reeking mouth the full width of the bulbous head opened and puckered and slavered. Ramses, deranged with fright, could only fall upon his knees in supplication to the filthy thing in the water.

"I implore You, mighty Glaaki, spare the life of one who—"

But behind him, the insectoid clicking and buzzing continued. *I will have his body*, one of the beetles seemed to be saying, while the other responded: *No, I will have it*. Then, in an incredible access of pain that filled Ramses' head nearly to bursting, the mental voices coalesced:

There is no time, the thing from the lake is going to take him, we must both possess him and project ourselves away.

Ramses wheeled around to see the shiny black beetles eyeing him with a terrifying intensity, but the vast pulpy shape from the lake was nearly upon him as well, and in one cataclysmic moment it all happened.

It was colossal, incomprehensible, outrageous. He was being swallowed up by the obscene thing that thrashed in the lake, yet he was being pulled in other directions too. He was still conscious of existence, but his thoughts were blended with, modulated by, interspersed with other strains of thought as if a plethora of minds were commingled in one being, minds that jointly—but separately as well—watched the scene beside the lake vanish in a blur of impressions, as if in rapid movement through some abysmal channel, whereupon a new scene took form, a scene in which desert sands stretched all around, sands dotted with mesquite bushes and gray clumps of sagebrush under a moonlit sky. Nearby, a huge Indian mound rose mesa-like from the desert floor, and beneath this mound a curious rumbling seemed to be starting, like something waking, something beginning to stir. Beyond the mound, the distant lights of a town shimmered on the horizon: Binger, Oklahoma. In the sands under the mound, the deep rumbling continued, as if some primal entity were about to shamble forth. But something new and inexplicable was making its ghastly way across the desert plain already.

Aside from one startled rattlesnake that slithered back down its hole at the thing's approach, the only witnesses to the arrival were probably lizards. To any human observer, had there been one, the vast shape that appeared out of nowhere and began moving through the night would have looked so bizarre that the brain, the eye, would have rejected it outright. Parts of its finny, leprous surface seemed admixed genetically with hints of insectoid shape, vague jumbled suggestions of clacking mandibles and spasmodically twitching legs, though in its slow but inexorable progress across the chaparral, the thing more nearly rolled than walked.

But the worst part would have been—to any observer prepared to understand it—that embedded in the purulent nightmare of its surface on one side, the shambling thing contained a surreal likeness of the face of Khem-Bei Ramses, only it was many, many yards across.

Part Four: Beyond the Wall of Time
by Brian McNaughton

JEFF COMBS WAS ENGROSSED IN HIS BATTERED PAPERBACK of *Interview with the Shaman*, by Kermit Armitage, when thunder burst right over the hospital. It damn near knocked him off the toilet.

He'd lost his place, but finding it again was no problem. He'd read the book at least five times. The very passage he'd been re-reading had been highlighted in yellow:

I hesitated to drink this stronger infusion of stramonium, but Gray Eagle was insistent: "You must drink without fear. The Hounds of Tyndalos will sense your fear in the windy spaces between souls or in the waste times beyond millennia."

"I can't," I said. "They'll know I'm afraid."

"Perhaps they already do," Gray Eagle said. "They are not confined to the astral plane. They may burst in upon us even here, unseen, unheard, like a plague, but infinitely more terrible, a plague of the spirit."

Impelled by his urgency, I drank, and I instantly knew I had been fatally poisoned. But no, this was worse than death. A comet had descended from heaven to atomize my body and soul, I was being raped by a supernova, I was at once torn and burned and scattered . . .

. . . only to find myself slammed together in the body of Klarkash-Ton, a philosopher in the court of High Atlantis, where—

The bathroom door rattled under a furious fist. "Combs!" It was Nurse Johnstone.

"Shit," he muttered, but she heard,

"Yes, Combs, that's what the lavatory is for, but that's not what you've been doing for the past hour and a half, is it?"

"I have this stomach bug," he called, hastily pulling up his pants and wondering how to conceal the book. And it would have to be concealed. She suspected he was studying Hustler or some such, but to be discovered with this perfectly respectable paperback would be far worse. Dr. Wagner had warned him against prying into the patient's former life and "encouraging his delusions."

He bloused out his white uniform shirt, planning to hide the book there, but he'd forgotten the vial already tucked in a knot in the shirt-tail. He swore as it clattered to the floor.

"What the hell—" The nurse's voice was drowned out by a second peal of thunder.

He examined the little bottle. No harm done. He'd been astounded when he learned that Jimson weed, something he'd associated with coyotes and cowpokes, actually grew in the swamps of Massachusetts, and that it was the same Datura stramonium prescribed by Gray Eagle. He'd gathered a plastic kitchen-bag of seeds and leaves and flowers, mashed them, brewed them on his hotplate in a borrowed lobster-steamer, strained the broth through paper towels and boiled it down to two ounces of brown liquid, which should be strong enough to send the whole population of Boston back to Atlantis.

This time he just stuck the vial in his pocket, The book—he hated to do it, but while Nurse Johnstone was hammering again, he slid the lid off the toilet-tank and dropped it in. He could retrieve it and dry it out later. Maybe he wouldn't need to read it again, once he'd actually journeyed beyond the stars and the centuries with the two greatest minds of the twentieth century.

Even so, he felt a deep sense of sacrilege. *Interview with the Shaman* would one day be revered as the Bible is now. Every word of it was true, and every page vital to humanity's continued existence.

He flushed the toilet and opened the door.

"Sounds like you dropped your crack-vial," the nurse said, alarmingly close to the truth. She frisked him, using only her hawk's eyes and bloodhound's nose. She was up to all the inmates' tricks, and she regarded attendants as a more contemptible subspecies of inmate.

"What's that in your pocket?" she demanded.

His heart stopped. She'd caught him. But she meant his other pocket. He pulled out a wadded handkerchief, some keys and change, dropping the coins and stooping for them to distract her.

"What did you think, that I was glad to see you?" he said to distract her further.

"You're not going to last much longer around here, not with your attitude, mister!" she snapped, but he believed she wasn't entirely displeased.

"Is something the matter? You need me?"

"This weather. In the old days, before meds really worked, this place would be a madhouse on a night like this," she giggled shrilly at her inadvertent joke. "But they're all a bunch of little lambs tonight. All except your special pal, Armitage. You did medicate him, right?"

"Just like it says on the chart."

"Well, he's been having one of his four-way arguments with himself all evening." She shuddered. "Blocky seems to be winning."

Glaaki, you moron, he wanted to say, but of course he didn't.

"Check on him, will you? I can't stand to look at him. Or smell him. But I have doctor's authorization to shoot him full of Thorazine if the oral dose doesn't work." She called after him, "And button your shirt, Combs! I know it's hard to tell the difference, but this is not a mosh-pit."

Glaaki certainly did seem to be winning, Jeff determined as soon as he unlocked the heavy door to the "Disturbed" wing and was assaulted by a roar that seemed unlikely to have emanated from any human throat. But the man was made of rubber: considering how widely he could open his mouth in his "Glaaki" phase, incredibly exhaling a stench of putrid fish, it was no surprise that he could expand his lungs like the bellows of an organ.

Of course if you believed Kermit Armitage, he was stuck between dimensions, and on a different but nearby plane he was largely composed of an amphibious abomination called Glaaki . . .

Whatever one chose to believe, Armitage was a phenomenon. According to Dr. Wagner, multiple personality disorder was a neurotic contrivance, and Armitage was the only paranoid schizophrenic in his experience who had ever exhibited the syndrome. Unlike other cases, his personalities weren't sequential. They were always present, fighting for control of his body.

Supermarket tabloids inclined more toward alien abduction theories. Armitage had disappeared in 1975 at the height of his popular success, to the intense relief of his colleagues at Harvard, who regarded his books about his conversations with a Native American shaman named Gray Eagle as an embarrassment to the university and to anthropology. Most scholars damned them as a pack of lies, a shameless pandering to the drug-crazed hippie anarchists who were then hammering at the gates of their button-down, ivy-covered sequestration.

Armitage had left the university hastily, claiming that Gray Eagle had died in Oklahoma, and that certain ceremonies must be performed over the body to prevent a malignant entity from conquering the earth. His colleagues were not terribly surprised when he vanished without a trace, especially since he was at the time awaiting trial on a charge of distributing psilocybin to some of his grad students.

Much as the university would have liked to sweep his memory under the rug, it was kept alive by the hippie anarchists, even after most of them had evolved into sedate New Agers. His books never went out of print, and it stirred a ripple of small headlines when, twenty years later, Kermit Armitage himself was discovered writhing in the throes of an apparent seizure at an Indian burial mound near Binger, Oklahoma.

They didn't know who he was at first—just "some loony who tried to bite my head off," in the words of an Oklahoma state trooper—but his fingerprints matched those of the missing professor, a fugitive still wanted by the FBI. Sent to question him, most reporters retreated in despair, although a rather bizarre interview saw print in Rolling Stone.

Reporters and police alike were baffled by one apparent anomaly: that although Armitage had been forty-nine years of age at the time of his disappearance, he now appeared to be no older. The doctors, however, refused to be baffled. Although granting his extraordinarily good physical shape for a man nearing seventy, they insisted that the determination of age was not an exact science.

Equally puzzling was the man's insistence—most of the time—that he was Khem-Bei Ramses, a British subject of Egyptian parentage, and, appropriately enough, a writer of weird fiction. It was suspected that he might have created and assumed this identity during his long absence, since such a person had indeed recently gone missing in England, but photographs of Ramses bore no resemblance at all to Armitage. It was more likely, anonymous police sources theorized, that the fugitive drug-guru had murdered the missing author. In his present condition, however, he was far beyond the reach of justice.

Just how far was obvious to Jeff Combs when he slid back the panel on the little, barred window to his padded cell. "Zkafka" and "Kzweig," as the inmate referred to his right and left hands, twitched and wriggled furiously, snapping their fingers in angry debate, while the head—Ramses, presumably—drooped wearily. A sonorous and ominous rumbling might have been continued thunder beyond the walls, but Jeff suspected Glaaki was responsible.

"Professor?" Jeff called softly.

"My dear fellow, I have told you time and again that I am not a professor of anything, flattering as your use of that honorific may be. I implore you once again to contact the British embassy in Washington—"

"No, Mr., Ramses, I'm sorry, I have to talk to Professor Armitage. Please, look, I didn't give you your meds. I haven't put you in restraints. Can't you return the favor by at least making an effort?"

"Zkafka" perked up, not unlike an attentive hand-puppet: in this case, a hand without a puppet. "Kzweig" writhed and twitched more furiously.

"Speak to me in English, professor, it does no good to point your antennae at me."

"Oh, bother!" said Ramses. The face rearranged itself into a less petulant look. Eerily, it continued to rearrange itself until the features changed. The skin-tone and even the eye-color seemed to lighten. Meanwhile, the right hand flopped to the floor as if suddenly paralyzed.

"What is it now, Combs?" The formerly British accent was now flat, hard Yankee, with a slight Ivy League overlay, "You can have no conception of the importance of the discussion you are interrupting—"

"I do have a conception, professor, really, I do. I read the interview you gave in—could you shut Glaaki, up, please?"

The inmate's face knotted. His stomach made a singularly disgusting gurgle. Could any human willfully make such noises with his digestive tract? Glaaki stopped roaring.

"What interview?"

"I've told you—well, I guess you were medicated when I told you."

"And I'm not, now. Yes, I guess I do owe you something for that. None of us can think straight with those confounded drugs in our system. But it's vitally important that I confer with Kzweig—"

"With Gray Eagle, you mean," Jeff said, and Armitage nodded thoughtfully. "In the interview, you said that you discovered the ancient city of

Kuen-Yian beneath the Indian mound. And you found Gray Eagle, the last survivor of that civilization. The rest of the population had projected their minds far, far into the future to take over a race of intelligent beetles."

"And we followed them," Armitage said with a touch of bitterness. "Gray Eagle wasn't truly of Kuen-Yian, you know, he was a reptilian creature from Yoth. I think he was trying to exact his vengeance on them, on me, on every being and on every age he could reach—"

"No!" Jeff cried as Armitage's left hand leaped to his throat in an apparent effort at self-strangulation. He croaked helplessly as his face darkened and his eyes bulged. Glaaki roared again. But how could that being roar, when the man's windpipe was cut off?

Against regulations and his better judgment, Jeff unlocked the door and plunged into the cramped, foul-smelling cell to seize Armitage's left hand and pry it from his throat. The attendant's strength was taxed to the fullest in an effort to restrain the hand of a frail scholar at least twenty-five years his senior.

At last Armitage could whoop for air. "Oh—my—God! Thank you, thank—Kzweig! By God, sir, I'll cut you off! I'll chew you off, if I have to. Lie still, man."

The hand did as it was told. Warily, Jeff withdrew his aching fingers.

"You seem to . . . ah . . . have the upper hand now," Jeff marveled.

"You are surprised? It's true, Gray Eagle, Kzweig, or whatever unpronounceable name he used while slithering around the depths of Yoth, has great powers. But now that we have shared the same body, the same mind, I possess those powers, too. And I am a human being, which still counts for something . . . "

"What are you staring at?" Jeff asked.

"Forgive me. Those tattoos of yours. They look oddly familiar." The skulls and demons Jeff had acquired during the height of his Heavy Metal phase were supposed to be unsettling to outsiders, but the professor was the first person who had ever seemed truly horrified by them. Armitage at last averted his eyes as he said, "It's nothing, never mind."

"Anyway," Jeff said, "you have to warn the world that Tulu, the being, the god, whatever, that brought the people of Kuen-Yian to earth in the first place, is in danger of rising from his eternal sleep, with horrible consequences for the human race."

"The human race will not be the only thing to suffer, young man. The result will be universally disastrous."

"And of course no one will believe you. They believe you're crazy even before you try telling them this story."

"Tact, obviously, is not—" The inmate sighed and moderated his tone: "No, of course, you're right."

"Then why don't you get out of this body? You've made jumps before, tremendous leaps into the future. Why not go back into the past and give yourself some breathing room while you figure out a way to alert people?"

"I can do that now as well as Gray Eagle could—better, perhaps. After all, it was that stupid reptile who transported us to England as a couple of giant cockroaches . . . "

Armitage paused to stare at his left hand, as did Jeff, but it accepted that judgment without so much as a twitch.

"But do you know what it requires?" Armitage said.

"Absolute internal peace, total concentration, iron self-discipline— things that simply cannot be achieved when one is sharing a body with three other creatures, even without being deadened and disoriented by psychoactive drugs. If you knew the thoughts even now squirming in Glaaki's vile mind . . . "

"What if you had the *right* psychoactive drugs? The sort of drug that enabled you to project your mind back to the court of Kull of Atlantis?"

"Mescaline, you mean, or . . . " Armitage's voice trailed off as he stared at the vial of muddy fluid Jeff had withdrawn from his pocket.

"Yes," Jeff said, "Jimson weed. I've read your books, professor, I've memorized your books, I've even taken the drugs, I've tried—"

"Combs!" The voice of Nurse Johnstone rang down the corridor. "What the hell are you doing in there, Combs?"

"I want to go with you!" Jeff cried in desperation. "I want to stride through the glorious boulevards of Atlantis, I want to descend into the red-litten depths of Yoth, I want to see the beings of Yuggoth take wing—"

"Then give me the damned bottle!" Armitage snapped, seizing it with his left hand and unstoppering it with his teeth. He drank.

"Good Lord," he said, shivering as he proffered the remainder to Jeff. "Hold onto me, and—"

Jeff drank and clutched the inmate. At the same time the left hand, the Gray Eagle hand, ripped open Armitage's shirt. Jeff felt something writhe wetly against his chest. He was reluctant to let go of the professor, but he was forced to pull back from a contact that nauseated him.

It took him a moment to grasp what he was looking at: a broad face that covered Armitage's chest and belly, an inhuman face that opened its mouth impossibly wide. Now he knew how Glaaki could roar without using the professor's mouth, but that knowledge did him no good as the left hand seized his neck in a steely grip and forced his head into the jaws of the beast.

◆   ◆   ◆

Kermit Armitage might have wept for his deliverer as he was torn loose from time and hurled into the void, but his own plight left room for no emotion but fear. The infusion had been far too strong.

But at least, and at long last, he was alone. The drug had blown apart his compound personality, No more would he hear the sibilant insinuations of Gray Eagle inside his own mind, no more would he cower at the bellowing of Glaaki, no more would he endure the fatuities of that quasi-English twit.

And he suddenly came to himself in the blinding brilliance of real time and space, enclosed in a box of glass and metal that was hurtling down a rutted road at a speed far in excess of any envisioned by road-builders with ox-carts in mind. Dark, thick woods rushed by, a blur until the bloated bole of a giant oak loomed before him in dreadful, discrete clarity.

"No! Not like this!" he shrieked as the world exploded in a red flash and a crashing of metal.

Armitage looked cautiously around him, patted himself down without finding any broken bones. He was wearing a shiny and much-mended three-piece suit and an article of clothing he had only heard tell of, a detachable, celluloid collar. The brim had torn loose from the crown of his natty new boater, which he had held in his lap, but that seemed the only damage. Except to the machine.

"Not like what?" said his companion.

"Not in a stupid automobile accident, I meant to say. I see that motoring is a skill not held in much esteem by the reptile-men of Yoth."

"*Reptile-men of Yoth*? Same to you, Grandpa, with bells on. It's only a stinking Ford. Maybe Daddy will see reason now and buy me a Stutz."

Armitage alighted, dusted himself while studying the other guardedly, "You aren't . . . Kzweig, are you?"

"Only if you want me to be," the driver simpered.

Armitage pulled his straw suitcase from the rumble-seat while he tried to gather his thoughts and assess his surroundings. Although this sort of car had been old-fashioned when he was a boy, it looked—or it had looked, before the crash—brand new. He might have ample time to warn the world of Tulu's awakening.

But if the obnoxious teen-ager who had wrecked the car was his grandson . . . He studied the hand gripping the weighty suitcase and found it unlined and unspotted. Probing a new stock of unfamiliar memories, he learned that the man whose body he now inhabited was in his thirties, though called "Grandpa" for his fuddy-duddy ways by the youths whose friendship he cultivated. He was the sort of man who had packed a suitcase full of books for a pleasure-trip.

Odd thoughts tugged at the corners of his mind, snatches of poetry, queer little fantasies of fairy-tale worlds. His new body belonged to a self-educated literary dilettante, a writer of unbounded unsuccess. Perhaps Armitage could harness the skills he had willy-nilly absorbed during his enforced intimacy with Khem-Bei Ramses to improve an his host's small talent. He might use fiction to alert the world of the danger it faced.

"It looks as if we'll have to throw ourselves on the mercy of those inbred Yankee degenerates you've been telling me about," his companion said as he pulled himself out of the wreckage. "I saw a farm about a mile back. I'm sure a telephone just isn't in the picture, and we'll be stuck here overnight. Only you'll have to sleep with the farmer's daughter."

Armitage's new host found such lewd innuendo extremely distasteful; and so now did Armitage.

Tagging behind the youth, he thought of another young man he had seen recently . . . if fifty-some years in the future counted as "recent." He recalled the hospital attendant's tattoos, and how they had matched those of a headless body atop a burial mound in Oklahoma. We had found that adult's body, of course, when Jeff Combs could have been no more than five years old. Beheaded by Glaaki, seized by the unspeakable Hounds that rampaged through the interstices of the Einsteinian continuum and delivered at some time in the remote past to the sadists of Kuen-Yian as a zombie slave . . . he shuddered. But he couldn't help hoping that Gray Eagle and Glaaki had met similar fates.

"Jeepers creepers, get a load of Reuben!" his companion whispered. "You don't suppose he manages to find time for a little cannibalism along with the obligatory incest and demonolatry, do you?"

Armitage looked up at the lank rustic who had paused in his scything to stare at them with feral and deeply suspicious eyes. The farmhouse behind him could have been built no later than the 1680s, and it surely hadn't been painted since then. He noted the small-paned windows, the contiguous congeries of outbuildings, speculated that it had all been put together with wooden pegs. He was surprised to be excited by such architectural speculations, but that was apparently the way of his new host. He began to imagine that such details might be used in a story; a horror story, of course.

"Forgive us for interrupting your work, sir," his companion said, displaying unsuspected good manners as he walked up to greet the intimidating farmer.

"Ayuh? Year machine had itself a mishap, eh? When I heerd the crash, I thought another one of them rocks had fell out of the sky. You boys hail from the city?"

"Yes, indeed, We were traveling to Quebec for a scholarly tour, I'm Harley Warren, and this—"

Warren and the farmer stared at Armitage, who had gasped. The sound was pitifully inadequate for the horror he felt, but it was all he could manage now that his host, merely stunned by the accident, came to life and reasserted control of his body and mind.

A drastic sense of unreality overwhelmed the professor, as if his awareness of the world were being muffled by a winding-sheet of irrational fancies. Remembering the experience of his leap into the body of a far-future being, he feared that he would henceforth be able to communicate with his host only through dreams, which might be ignored, dismissed or simply forgotten. Fighting to leave an imprint of his precious knowledge, he mentally babbled the words *Tulu . . . Yoth . . . N'Kai . . . wgah'nagl . . .* and heard them degenerate into the nonsensical tongue of the subconscious.

His host hardly noticed, for the farmer's words had touched one of his special enthusiasms and seized his full attention. He demanded, "You say a rock fell out of the sky, sir?"

Used to his companion's quirky and absent-minded ways, young Warren sighed and pressed on with his introduction: "And this is my friend, Mr. Lovecraft."

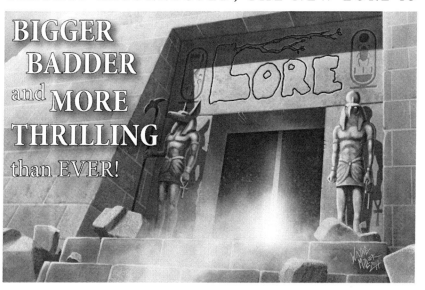

CPSIA information can be obtained at www.ICGtesting.com
Printed in the USA
BVOW080133221111

276503BV00001B/7/P